LETHAL ACTION

LETHAL ACTION

Danger in the Deep South

RACHEL DYLAN

Lethal Action
Copyright © 2015 by Rachel Dylan

ISBN: 9781519762658

NYLA Publishing
350 7th Avenue, Suite 2003, NY 10001, New York.
http://www.nyliterary.com

Be strong and of a good courage, fear not, nor be afraid of them: for the Lord thy God, he it is that doth go with thee; he will not fail thee, nor forsake thee.
Deuteronomy 31:6

ACKNOWLEDGEMENTS

Many thanks to my amazing agent, Sarah E. Younger, who is a constant source of support and encouragement. I'd also like to thank everyone at the Nancy Yost Literary Agency, including Natanya Wheeler for all of her assistance.

CHAPTER ONE

Five years. Hope Finch was celebrating her fifth year anniversary as an attorney at the prestigious New York law firm of Rice and Taylor by chugging down another cup of lukewarm coffee. She'd lost count at mug number six. As a fifth year associate, she still had a lot to prove. Not only to the firm, but to herself as well.

She glanced at the clock on her computer screen and saw that she'd worked late into the night and skipped dinner again. Nothing unusual for her. The Wakefield trial was taking up all of her time—and then some. But there was no way she was going to say she couldn't handle the workload. As a midlevel associate, she should be able to run with the big boys. Or at least pretend like she could. If that meant coffee would be her only source of sustenance then so be it. If she wanted to make partner within three years, then she had to stick to the game plan.

Hope shutdown her computer and grabbed her laptop bag embroidered with the bright red R&T logo. It was very possible she'd still put in a little bit more time working tonight at home. Also part of her normal routine.

The big New York City law firm was relatively quiet for a weeknight. Only a couple of other associates were working away in their offices. She felt a tiny shred of guilt for leaving, but then quickly dismissed it. She was still on track for getting all of her work done in time for trial and sleep was necessary. She couldn't afford to make any mistakes right now. There was too much on the line. Both for her client and for her.

When the cold winter New York air blew against her face, she was glad to be headed home to her cozy apartment. It cost her a good chunk of her lawyer salary, but it was worth it. She paid a hefty price to be close to her office, and she still lived in a five hundred foot box.

Cinching her pink pea coat tightly around her waist, she walked quickly down the dark street. Even at this hour, there were still plenty of people walking around. She loved the anonymity and hustle and bustle of the city. It gave her the freedom she felt like she'd earned. She never understood how people could live in small towns where everyone knew every detail about your life. If she had it her way, no one would know anything about her. Except what she chose to share with them.

When she arrived at her high-rise apartment door, she turned the key in the lock, and dropped her bag on the floor. Immediately, she kicked off her tall heels and unbuttoned her grey suit jacket. Home sweet home. It wasn't much, but it was hers, and for that she was proud.

She started to reach for the light switch but a strong hand grabbed her wrist throwing her off balance. She screamed as her pulse thumped wildly. The hand moved to her mouth and the other wrapped securely around her waist pulling her into him. The intruder stood behind her, and she couldn't see him.

This was it. This man was going to kill her. He was strong. She was no match for him. In that moment, she found herself clicking back through the events of her life like a movie reel. Her horrible childhood front and center. Not enough time to make all of her dreams come true and to fully recover from her past. Wondering how much time she still had left. And filled with regret. She fought harder.

"Stop struggling. I'm not here to hurt you," he said. "I'm Special Agent Gabe Marino. I'm a federal agent. I work for the FBI."

The FBI? What was an FBI agent doing in her apartment? She didn't believe him, so she kept fighting. She bit down hard on his hand, and he let out a groan. Unfortunately, he didn't let go. Not willing to give up, she gathered up her strength and stomped on his foot.

Nothing was working though.

"Listen to me, Ms. Finch. I am going to drop my arms and step away from you. Don't scream." He slowly pulled his hand away from her mouth and loosened his grip. Then he turned on the lights, and she got her first look at her assailant. He was tall with short dark hair and chocolate colored eyes. He wore a dark suit and a striped navy tie. He looked the part of an FBI agent, but he could be anyone.

"Here, let me show you." He slowly reached into his suit jacket and pulled out his credentials. He showed her his FBI badge and identification.

His identification looked legitimate, but she also knew it was easy to forge credentials if you had the right resources. She didn't believe him yet. "Why would an FBI agent resort to breaking and entering?" she asked.

"I didn't break into your apartment. Actually, I have a warrant." He reached into his pocket and handed it to her. "Go ahead, take a look."

She didn't want to take her eyes off of him, but she glanced down quickly and read the warrant. This guy might actually be legitimate. The fact that he hadn't hurt her yet added to his credibility. But what if he was trying to gain her trust only to hurt her? Hadn't she had enough struggles in her life?

"What do you want with me?"

He stood with his hands in his pockets. "Information. I need to know what your involvement is with Carlos Nola."

She took a step back providing her a little distance. "Mr. Nola is a board member of Wakefield Corporation. My biggest client at Rice and Taylor. Or I guess I should say that Wakefield Corporation is technically a client of my firm. Not me specifically. I work on their cases. Have since I started working there."

"I know that."

"If you know so much about me, then why did you have to break into my apartment? Why not set up a meeting with me at the firm?"

"Because I needed to be discreet. I'm working on a very sensitive case."

"I don't understand what you're after here." She looked up into his dark eyes and wondered what was really going on. If he was really FBI and asking questions about her client, that couldn't be good. He definitely had her attention.

"We can do this the easy way or the hard way, Ms. Finch."

She crossed her arms not appreciative of his bossy tone. "I'm not saying another word, Mr. Marino, until you explain why you're really here. If you really are a federal agent then you know that I can't reveal privileged information about my firm's client, Wakefield Corporation."

"It's not Wakefield I'm that interested in. At least not directly. It's Carlos Nola. Like I said, I have a reasonable suspicion that you're involved with him and his questionable business practices. You'll get much more leniency if you work with us rather than if you try to protect him. So let me help you."

Could this really be happening? What was Nola involved in that was getting this scrutiny from the FBI? "Mr. Nola lives in Georgia. I've worked with him, and met him about five or so times in person, and every single time he was entirely professional. I would like to help you, but I really have no idea what you're talking about. He's a legitimate businessman. Respected in his community."

"This is about what is going on in his community—Maxwell, Georgia. That's where Wakefield's home office is."

"I'm well aware of that," she shot back. She wasn't telling this suit anything. She wasn't guilty, so that led her to believe that he was purely on a fishing expedition. She'd worked enough government investigations of big corporations to sense when there was actual evidence. If he had solid evidence he certainly wouldn't be hounding her.

"And you're sure there's nothing you want to tell me?" He took a step toward her.

"How do I even know you're from the FBI? For all I know you work for Cyber Future."

"Ah." He smiled. "No, I'm definitely a federal agent. How is the litigation between Wakefield and Cyber Future going?"

"That is not your concern, Mr. Marino. Now I'm going to have to ask you to leave my apartment."

"Are you sure you want to do that?"

"Yes. Please leave."

He cocked his head to the side. "If you are innocent, it's in your best interest not to say we had this conversation with anyone at your law firm. And if you're working with Nola, you're in danger. So don't say that you haven't been officially warned. This conversation isn't over, though. We'll be speaking again soon."

Before she could say anything he turned and walked out of her door.

"No, we won't," she said to out loud to herself.

What should she do? Should she tell the partners at the firm? No. First, she needed to figure out what was really going on. And that's exactly what she planned to do. If she went to her supervising partner at the firm right now he might pull her off the case. So she'd have to get to the bottom of this on her own. A constant theme of her life.

The litigation between Wakefield and Cyber Future had gotten ugly. The breach of contract case should have been all business and routine, but it had gotten personal between both the executives and the lawyers representing the two companies. Cyber Future wanted to take down her client. Cyber Future was quickly becoming a competitor of Wakefield. Was Cyber Future behind this FBI inquiry? She certainly wouldn't put it past them. Cyber Future was out for blood.

***

Gabe Marino wrapped his navy scarf tightly around his neck and let out a deep breath. Hope Finch knew that he didn't have a solid case against her. Even getting the warrant was difficult. She put on a good show that was for sure. When she looked at him with her big brown eyes and played dumb, he almost believed her. She would have most people fully believing her innocence, but she'd been working with Nola for five years. She admitted that much herself.

He'd been watching her for the past few days. All she did was go back and forth from the office keeping very long hours. It didn't even appear that she even took a lunch break. He pictured her eating some microwavable meal at her desk and drinking coffee made in a fancy espresso machine purchased by the law firm.

He hadn't really known what to expect. Her file had made clear that she was a rising star at Rice and Taylor. She'd graduated top of her law school class. Obviously smart. She was also an attractive woman. Not that he was taking particular note of that. Every time he'd seen her over the past few days she'd worn her long blonde hair pulled back in a low ponytail. Her suits looked expensive. Maybe even designer. But he wasn't surprised given that she worked at one of the most prestigious law firms in the city and had the stellar salary to match. She would need to look the part. Her salary made his look laughable. It irked him that big firm lawyers were so grossly overpaid as they defended massive corporations. Meanwhile, federal agents who often put their lives on the line were often barely making ends meet.

He had a job to do, and he couldn't help the feeling that Hope was right in the middle of it all. He didn't believe in coincidences. Too many unanswered questions made him uneasy. Was she part of the plot that Nola was cooking up, or was she in potential danger? Gabe believed that Nola was running several illegal businesses in Maxwell using Wakefield resources to help him. Those businesses included drug trafficking and money laundering. All things that had no place in Maxwell.

As he walked to his hotel, he tried to focus. The cold New York City weather was messing with his brain. He could never live up there, and he couldn't get back to Georgia soon enough.

This case was personal for him. He worked in the Atlanta field office of the FBI, but he was born and raised in Maxwell, Georgia. And he planned to always live there. The commute to Atlanta was forty five minutes. But it was well worth the drive and extra gas to live in Maxwell and maintain his quiet lifestyle. A lifestyle that was threatened by people like Carlos Nola.

There was something sinister going on in his town—the town he loved. And he intended to stop it. Hope Finch might be the key to unraveling the entire mystery. She knew more than she was letting on. She had to.

Carlos Nola was up to no good. Gabe knew that Nola was using Wakefield Corporation to help further his criminal enterprise that was infecting Maxwell. What he didn't know is if it was only Nola who was involved. How far did Nola's influence reach?

Hope had been telling the truth about her meetings with Nola. His research indicated that they'd met recently in New York and periodically at her firm before that. Even if she wasn't working for him as part of his criminal ventures, she could still be useful in his investigation. As one of the Wakefield lawyers, she'd have unprecedented access to Nola. He wasn't giving up on her. There was still a lot of work to do. And Hope Finch was the center of it all.

***

Hope didn't know what to think when she'd gotten the email from her boss, Sam Upton, telling her that they needed to meet first thing in the morning. Sam was the partner in charge of the litigation between Wakefield and Cyber Future. Hope worried that she'd done something wrong. She recounted the work she'd completed over the past week. Nothing stood out in her mind that she could've messed up, but Sam was such an important partner at the firm she couldn't afford to make any mistakes. Not even a small one. If he removed her from the case, she'd be devastated.

She took a deep breath and smoothed down her suit jacket before walking to his office. His door was open, but she still knocked. Sam was nice enough to work for, but there was still a gulf between him being a partner and her being a mid-level associate. A pretty gigantic gulf—he held all the power, and she held none.

"Come in, Hope," he said. Sam wore a custom made navy suit and blue striped tie. He'd been working at the firm for decades, and his personal tailor often visited him at the office.

She started trying to figure out how to explain away whatever it was that she must have messed up.

"So," he said, "I've actually got some exciting news. Or at least I hope you'll think so because I do."

"Okay," she replied. Now he really had her attention.

"First, let me say that you've been doing great work on the Wakefield case. Really performing above your level and everyone has noticed including the client. They've been highly impressed with your dedication to this case. You've really been keeping this train on the tracks."

"Thank you, sir." She clasped her hands with nervous excitement.

"How many times have I told you not to sir me, Hope?"

"I'm sorry."

He smiled. "And stop apologizing. Just listen up for a minute. You know I was supposed to try this case with Harry. But there's been an emergency international arbitration for one of our biggest clients. Harry's on a plane to Brussels right now and won't be back for a couple of months. I decided to send him because they needed a partner over there right now with his international experience."

She started to try to process what all of this would mean. If Harry wasn't going to try the case with Sam, then who was?

He leaned forward in his chair. "Since you know the case so well, I want you to go to Maxwell, Georgia, and get us set up for trial next week. And then at trial you'll be second chair. My number two. Also means a literal seat at counsel's table and you examining and crossing select witnesses."

"Second chair?" She heard herself say the words out loud but couldn't fathom it.

"Yes, you've earned it. I know associates don't get much trial experience around here since our cases have such a high dollar value. So you need to take this one head on. You'll be working with our local counsel in Maxwell to prepare for trial. I'll be coming down there in a few days, but I want you on the ground now. You up for this?"

She didn't even know how to respond. "Of course I am." This is exactly what she wanted. What she'd been working so hard for five years at the firm to show that she had what it takes to make it in big law. This was her time to shine.

"Great. Now have your secretary book you a flight for this afternoon. Get out of here and pack. I want you on a plane and in Maxwell by this evening."

She nodded realizing it was probably better not to start gushing to her boss. "Thank you, I won't let you down."

She remained calm until she got back to her office and shut the door. Then she let out a squeal as she hopped around her small office. Second chair! And getting to go to Maxwell ahead of Sam to work with the client and the local law firm. This was a once in a career opportunity for someone like her. She hadn't felt this happy in years. If ever.

She couldn't let this chance slip away. She'd have to be on the top of her game the entire time. While Sam cared about all of his clients, he'd been college roommates with Lee Wakefield, the CEO of Wakefield Corporation. So Sam took this case personally. He wouldn't accept anything but her best—and then some. She'd proven herself to be a hard worker, and it was nice to see that it was actually paying off. But her work was far from done.

Hope gave her secretary instructions on booking the flight to leave New York around lunchtime and then went home to pack. She'd never been to Georgia. Much less the small town of Maxwell. This would be an experience she'd never forget. And there was also an added bonus. Now she could ensure she wouldn't run into agent whatever his name was again. Their altercation last night was strange, and it bothered her that he was making allegations against Carlos Nola.

A tiny shred of doubt crept into her thoughts. What if the FBI agent was right and Nola was involved in some illegal activity? Could her work actually be protecting and aiding a criminal? No. She refused to believe that.

She'd had a few meetings with Nola in New York, and he always seemed entirely professional. Friendly, a gentleman, and with a shrewd business acumen. There had never been any hint of impropriety in any of their discussions. She'd spoken to him on the phone quite a bit lately because of trial preparation, and she'd experienced no red flags of any kind. Wakefield Corporation was also a very well thought of business with board members who were highly respected in the community. No, there simply had to be some mistake on the FBI's part.

The FBI was mistaken, and it was her job to protect her client, Wakefield Corporation. Nola wouldn't do anything to jeopardize the business, because as a board member, he had a vested interest to stay above board with all of his business dealings.

She wasn't one to just sit back, though. She planned to find out what the FBI was really after before it was too late.

CHAPTER TWO

By the time Hope's flight touched down at the Atlanta airport, Hope was running on adrenaline. She'd almost felt sorry for herself for a couple of minutes when she realized how easy it was for her to just get up and jump on a plane with no notice. She didn't have a boyfriend, didn't have that many friends who would notice her absence. Not even a cat.

She was a loner and married to the firm. It was a sacrifice she had made with full knowledge of the costs. It was also one she made out of necessity. He was the first person she'd truly trusted. She was heartbroken over his deceit. Being alone was better than being hurt.

And now those sacrifices were going to pay off. She was going to be second chair. She was the one who was going to work this week with the client and local counsel in advance of trial. It was all worth it. It even helped put away some of the pain she'd been dealing with for the past year after Barry cheated on her. She'd had no choice but to leave him after that.

Hope and the rest of the legal team from the firm were staying at the best hotel in Maxwell. Or at least that's what she'd been told. When she pulled up her rental car into the lot, she let out a breath. She was not in New York anymore. Wow. Admittedly, she'd been spoiled because the other cases she traveled for were in big cities. Four and five star hotels were the norm—especially when a partner was involved.

But as she stared up at the hotel, she realized she needed to adjust her expectations. It was the Maxwell Inn. The big sign hung in between two large magnolia trees. Two of the biggest trees she'd ever seen.

She was here for trial anyway, not to go on a luxurious vacation. She'd just have to make it work. Hope hadn't grown up in a family with money so she knew how to adapt. It was Sam she started to worry about.

The word she'd really use to describe the inn was historic. It was only a few floors and looked more like an old southern mansion than a hotel. No doubt that they wouldn't have around-the-clock room service.

She parked her car—no valet that was for sure—and grabbed her two suitcases. Had she over packed? Yes. But the fear of not having something she needed had been too much to ignore, so she'd almost emptied her small closets.

The wind blew her hair into her face, but it wasn't the frigid wind she was so accustomed to. It was barely cool. She probably could've left her heavy dress coat back in her apartment. She assumed it would still get cold in Georgia in January, but she was almost sweating under her clothes as she walked into the hotel lobby to check in.

The lobby was larger than she expected, with hardwood floors and oil paintings hung on the walls. A woman with bleached blonde hair stood behind the check-in counter. She smiled broadly. "You checking in, ma'am?"

Her southern drawl was unmistakable.

"Yes, I am. I'm Hope Finch."

"And I'm Mary March, nice to meet ya. I spoke to someone at your law firm earlier today. We're ready for your entire group. The trial you're working on is all the talk in Maxwell."

"Really?" Hope would have to get used to the small town atmosphere where everyone knew everything about everyone.

She'd grown up in New York City. Anonymity was one of the things that helped get her through her childhood.

"Of course. And all you have to do while you're here is let people know that you're one of Wakefield's lawyers, and you'll get the extra special treatment."

"Thanks for the tip."

Mary smiled as she flipped through the paperwork that spit out of the printer. "We take care of our own in Maxwell. Even turned down the other side's lawyers when they called to make a reservation. Let them stay at the motel off old country road. Wakefield is one of the biggest employers for the city. We don't take too kindly to being sued by a fancy California company on some trumped up charges. We depend on Wakefield here in Maxwell. So you and your team can count on the town of Maxwell to take care of you."

"We'll do our best."

"We have you in room two thirty two. You're in one of our junior suites as requested. So you'll have a little work area. Here's your key. And just holler if you need anything, I'll be here until midnight. Then Jim takes over for the rest of the night."

"Great. Could you tell me where I could grab some dinner?"

"Oh, honey, you're in the south now. There are plenty of good options if you're willing to try them. Pa's Diner is only two blocks from here if you take a right out of the inn. Then just walk down the sidewalk and you can't miss it. They have everything you could want including an amazing breakfast. If you like barbeque, we got some of the best in the state at Maxwell Mel's BBQ—and don't tell Mel I said some of the best. Mel would insist that it is the best barbeque. It's just a block the other direction. Hang a left out of here. And finally, the best friend chicken you've ever had is served at Billy's Shack. But you'll need to drive there. It's about a mile or so down the way. Also, we will bring complimentary hot tea and coffee to your room. Just give us a call and we'll have it right up."

"Thank you. I appreciate it." Her mind was reeling at how she was going to fit in her suits if she ate fried food for every single meal.

But for now she couldn't stress about that. Hope felt her stomach rumble and knew that food was a must. The complimentary peanuts from the flight weren't sufficient. She took the elevator up one floor, rolling her bags along with her. She opened up her hotel room and was pleasantly surprised. No, it wasn't a fancy New York hotel room, but it looked clean and the bright light of the mild winter afternoon shone through. Covering the bed was a large lavender quilt. There was a small sitting and work area with a desk and chairs. A hint of lemon cleaner and cedar hung in the air. Quickly she put all her suits on hangers and unpacked the rest of her clothes in a hurry.

After a brief moment of deliberation, she decided to try the diner. Anyplace called Pa's was enough to intrigue her. She wouldn't even need a jacket for the short walk. She was already getting spoiled with the warmer weather.

She looked down the street at the various shops and stores. The research she had done on the town let her know that the area she was staying in was filled with cute shops and restaurants. About a mile or two out, the town was more commercialized with a lot of chains. Wakefield Corporation was a couple of miles away from the inn. She was anxious to see the company headquarters in person. That would come first thing in the morning. Tonight was all about getting settled in and having a good dinner.

She passed a few people on the street that all said hello. It wouldn't be long before the town would be abuzz about all the lawyers participating in the trial—especially the rival law firm from Silicon Valley. Cyber Future had hired the most notoriously ruthless law firm in the U.S. to represent them. The Jennings Law Firm out of California made billions on plaintiff's lawsuits. Some of very questionable merit. The lawyers didn't care about their clients, only about the cases that had the potential to bring them huge jury verdicts.

Aha, she thought to herself, when she saw Pa's up ahead on the right. The sign was in big bright red lettering. For once, she actually liked that the sidewalks weren't filled with people. It allowed her to really breathe. Something she hadn't done in a long time. She loved New York City and never wanted to leave. But maybe a visit to Maxwell, and this trial, was just what she needed to recharge and reinvigorate herself. The trial experience itself would be amazing. And the town seemed quiet and peaceful. Yeah, she would probably get a lot of attention since she was a lawyer for Wakefield, but she doubted anyone would really care about her as a person. Only about the lawsuit. So there was still an amount of anonymity that she craved.

She walked into Pa's Diner and bells jingled loudly on the door. Since she was having an early dinner, there weren't that many people there. A few people sat at the counter on high top swivel chairs and there were a couple of other people spread out in booths.

"Hello there. You can have a seat wherever you want," the tall, thin waitress said. Her brown hair was pulled back in a high ponytail, and she wore a t-shirt that said Pa's in big red letters.

Hope sat down at a booth by the window and the waitress walked over and set a menu in front of her. "I'm Mags. I'll be helping ya today." She paused and looked at her with a smile. "You must be here for the trial," she said.

"Am I that obvious?"

Mags laughed. "What's your name?"

"Hope Finch."

"What side?" She stood with her right hand on her hip.

"The home team." She couldn't help but smile.

"Well then in that case, let me tell you about the specials. We make a mean bacon cheeseburger. If that's too heavy for you, we do amazing breakfast food all day. Even do egg whites if you're into that type of thing."

Hope chuckled. She was so obviously a city girl. An omelet sounded awesome.

"How about a veggie omelet?"

"Great choice. That comes with toast and cheese grits. That okay?"

"Actually I've never had grits, but I'd love to try them."

"Perfect. You won't be disappointed. And what to drink?"

"Water is fine."

She shook her head. "Oh no, dear. I'll bring you a sweet tea. You have to try it, too. We make it the sweetest in town."

Hope knew better than to argue with the waitress. The last thing she needed to do was to make enemies before the sun went down on her first day in town. So she'd just try the sweet tea and hope that she could handle the excessive sugar. She even drank her coffee black.

Since Hope had grown up in New York, she was literally a city girl through and through. When Mags brought back the sweet tea and stood there waiting with a big grin, she had no choice. She took a big sip and felt the sweetness hit her tongue. It was surprisingly good but she wanted something extra. "Could I have some lemon to go with it?"

"Sure thing, hun. And your food will be out in just a few."

Hope let out a sigh and tried to get her head around all that was happening. She'd be meeting the local lawyers they were working with tomorrow. Since they were litigating this case outside of New York, they were required by law to have local lawyers. But there was no mistake who was in charge. Sam Upton was running the show. The local guys were just for dress and to play a purely supporting role. So far the local firm had been very helpful and even brought up great legal points on the team conference call. As long as everyone understood their various roles, Hope didn't foresee any problems.

"Can I have a seat," a deep male voice said.

She looked up. No way. It couldn't be. "What are you doing here?" She clenched her fists instantly on alert. This guy couldn't mess up her case. She refused to let him.

"That isn't a very nice way to greet your favorite FBI agent," he said softly. "But right now I'm not an agent." He gave her a look that made Hope grumble.

"You're not my favorite anything." She paused, her mind racing as she tried to assess the situation. Then she processed what he had said to her. "So you're undercover?"

"Yes, and I'd appreciate it if you didn't blow it."

She glanced up at him. "And what, are you stalking me now?"

"Of course not. I'm working. Just like you."

"And part of working is following me down to Maxwell, Georgia from New York?"

He smiled revealing a small dimple in his right cheek. "That's where you're wrong. I wasn't following you. I've got work here. Just like you do."

She couldn't believe what he was saying. "But you were just in New York City."

"Yes. I only flew up there to talk to you. I actually live in Maxwell."

Now things were getting very strange. She looked up into his dark chocolate eyes that looked even darker now with the light of the diner. As if she wasn't already suspicious of him after he basically broke into her apartment. And now he was living in the town that she was going to be staying in for the foreseeable future. Her gut was screaming at her that she needed to keep her guard up around this guy. While he had been talking about danger, he might actually be a threat to her.

"I do need to sit, though."

Before she could object, he sat down across from her.

"I've already told you everything I know," she said. "Which is pretty much nothing since there's nothing to tell."

"I'm taking on Carlos Nola. And I plan to do it with your help or not. But as I told you before, if we get evidence of your involvement with his schemes, the prosecutor will not go easy on you. You are an officer of the court after all. Think about your career. Not about protecting a criminal."

"And I told you, Mr. Marino, that I have absolutely nothing to hide. I'm a very good lawyer, and I work hard for my clients. But I have no basis to think that Mr. Nola or anyone at Wakefield Corporation is doing anything illegal. Calling him a criminal is slanderous. Don't think that we won't come after you and the FBI for harassment and slander. I'm sure I can come up with a number of other allegations to put in the complaint too."

"Once you see some of the evidence you might change your mind."

"What evidence?"

The waitress walked over and set down the large fluffy omelet in front of her. She took a moment just to breathe in the wondrous smell of veggies, cheese, and eggs.

"Hi, Gabe," the waitress said. "You want your usual?"

"Sure thing, Mags."

"And I see you met one of Wakefield's brightest lawyers. I told her we'd take good care of her while she was in town. Even got her drinking sweet tea already."

Hope couldn't help but smile. Mags seemed like a really nice lady. When Mags walked away, she turned her attention squarely back to Gabe. She didn't need this distraction right now. The trial started in less than a week.

She took a bite of her omelet but didn't break eye contact. She'd wait for him to make the next move.

"The evidence will be revealed to you when I can."

She laughed. "That's not nearly good enough, and you know that."

"I hear what you're saying, Ms. Finch, but I think you can probably understand that I can't take your word for it that you are oblivious to Nola's activities. I would have to put you in front of a grand jury. Who knows how that would impact your legal career."

"Wait." She dropped her fork down on her plate. "Are you threatening me?"

He leaned forward. "I'm simply advising you of your options."

"It certainly doesn't sound like that to me." She paused gathering her thoughts. "I don't care if you work for the FBI or any other federal government agency. You're not going to bully me. I've got a job to do. A multi-million dollar lawsuit to defend. And if you keep harassing me, I will report you to FBI headquarters. I'm not stupid enough to think that reporting you locally would do any good."

"Now wait a minute." He lifted up his hand. "I haven't harassed you. I had a warrant to search your apartment. And I have every right to be here at this diner right now."

"A flimsy very limited warrant that I read with great interest."

"Yes, but a warrant no less. And I told you. I live here. This is my town, and I'm going to do what I have to so that it's protected against men like Carlos Nola."

She crossed her arms. "You just don't like Carlos because he's an outsider who decided to move into your precious Maxwell."

"Where he's from has nothing to do with it. He's using Wakefield Corporation to do his dirty work. This town is a quiet, peaceful, and law abiding place. A place you can raise your kids and not be fearful. I won't let someone with ties to organized crime change that."

"Organized crime." Ah, now things were starting to become a bit more clear. This guy was trying to connect Nola. "Are you profiling him because he's Italian?"

"Hope." He used her name for the first time. "What kind of name do you think Marino is? My dad was Italian. Nola's heritage has nothing to do with it. But who he associates with is another story."

Mags walked back to the table and placed the biggest hamburger Hope had ever seen in front of Gabe. The bacon and cheese was practically exploding off of the burger. The shoestring French fries made her mouth water. She almost wished she had some to go with her omelet.

"Would you like a French fry?"

As much as she wanted one, she refused to take one from the enemy. "No, I'm good, thanks."

"Suit yourself. Just wait until you taste the barbeque and fried pickles down the street."

"Fried pickles? Are you serious?"

He dumped a healthy dose of ketchup on his plate. "Oh yeah. They come with a special dip. I'll take you there tomorrow."

She shook her head. "No. I have to work tomorrow. That's what I'm here to do, and you're not going to interfere with my trial preparation with your crazy theories not based upon any evidence."

"You're not going to get rid of me that easily."

"Watch me."

She was already tired of this annoying handsome federal agent. But what if he was right and there was something sinister going on in Maxwell? Even if there was, that didn't mean that Nola was involved. It did shatter her image of the town though. Should she be worried about her safety?

"Where you staying?" he asked.

"The Maxwell Inn."

"Maxwell's finest. A step down from your NYC lifestyle."

"You don't know me. So you shouldn't judge me."

"I wasn't judging. Just observing."

She'd had enough. This guy had no idea who she was, or where she'd come from. "I'm going to finish my omelet and go back to the inn." Was that a strong enough hint for him to back off?

"I'll walk you. And for your trouble, I'll pay for your dinner."

"No, I don't want to owe you anything, Mr. Marino."

"I wouldn't be a proper southern gentleman if I let you pay for your first meal in town."

She shrugged and picked up her fork again.

They ate in silence. She sighed knowing that this was a losing fight. She was having an internal battle. One side of her wanted to really dislike this guy. He'd intruded on her life—literally. Made unfounded accusations about one of the board members of her client.

But on the other hand, there was something about the entire situation—and him—that concerned her. She tried to push the feeling away, but she couldn't help but feel drawn to this man. And as a purely practical matter, she knew she couldn't get away from him. This was his town. He was on a mission.

Then it occurred to her. Maybe it would be better not to fight against him, but to figure out what he knew.

After all, she represented Wakefield. Not Carlos Nola. And if Carlos was engaging in any illegal activity, she had an ethical obligation as an attorney to protect the interests of Wakefield.

Mags walked back over to the table. "Dinner's on the house tonight, ya'll. Hope, we'd love to see you back again here anytime."

"Thank you, Mags. It was delicious."

Mags smiled and walked away.

"Let's get out of here then." He stood up from the table.

When they stepped outside, she was once again amazed by the mild air that blew against her face.

"So, you're working with the Trent Law Firm, right? They are the biggest firm in town. Not that any law firm in Maxwell is that big."

"Yes, with Greg Trent, the senior."

He nodded. "The founding partner, and fixture of this town. That was a smart move."

"We thought so."

She took leisurely steps down the sidewalk. The sun was starting to make its descent down behind the fluffy white clouds. She couldn't help but look in the store windows as they walked. A cute antique shop caught her eye, and she made a mental note to come back and visit at some point.

The short walk to the inn was over before she knew it. "This is me. Thanks for dinner. I can't help but think you had something to do with that."

"Anytime. And remember, you'll be seeing a lot of me."

She didn't have anything nice to say to that so she just turned around and walked into the inn.

When her head hit the pillow she was asleep almost immediately. The traveling and general excitement had worn her out. However, she had always been a light sleeper, and a sound awoke her in the middle of the night.

She sat up in the bed with a start, trying to regain her bearings. She was in Maxwell, not in her apartment in New York.

There, she heard it again. It sounded like someone was rattling the doorknob. Fear shot through her, and she jumped up out of the bed and grabbed her mace from her purse on the floor. The rattling noise continued. She gripped the mace tightly in her hand.

Weren't small towns supposed to be safe? Gabe's ominous words about Nola's criminal activities spreading into the town replayed in her head. She took a few deep breaths and debated about whether she should grab her phone and call 9-1-1. Maybe if she made a lot of noise the intruder would leave?

Her heart pounded and she listened. She waited. And waited. No sounds. Gaining a bit of courage she walked toward the door and looked out the peephole. Nothing.

Was her mind playing tricks on her? No. She'd heard something. Maybe it was someone who figured out they were trying to get into the wrong room?

Her peaceful night of slumber was no more. Feeling a bit worried, she took one of the chairs from the table and put it in front of the door. She looked at the clock and saw it was almost three a.m. Sleep wouldn't come easily again tonight.

CHAPTER THREE

G abe woke up and after one cup of coffee was ready to start his day. His house in Maxwell was perfect for him and his black Labrador Zeke. Recently adopted from the pound after his golden had passed away. After a brisk run with Zeke, he knew it was going to be a good day.

He thought back to Hope Finch and the look on her face when he'd told her about the fried pickles. Talk about city girl come down to the country. What was her involvement in this scheme? He'd found absolutely nothing to tie her to Nola. And his instincts told him that she was completely innocent.

The bigger issue was how was he going to take down Carlos Nola? How was he going to prove that Nola was behind the influx of crime in Maxwell? His best lead right now was Hope. Because even if she wasn't involved with Nola, she had the best access to him. If that meant shadowing her around town and conducting his investigation, he'd do just that.

He'd been given a great deal of latitude, thanks to closing his last case that had given his boss at the FBI in the Atlanta field office national recognition. When Gabe had stumbled upon what was going on in Maxwell, he begged his boss to let him take it on. He put on a detailed case and argued that he should be given the chance to determine what Nola was up to. His boss had agreed.

He'd have eyes and ears at the Trent Law Firm. Granted, he wouldn't have access to privileged material, but his family and the

Trent family went way back. Just like most families in Maxwell. One thing was true for most all in the town—the residents wanted to keep Maxwell safe. Gabe knew the influx of violent crime had to be linked to Nola's network. The money laundering and drug running business often turned ugly.

It was time to find Hope. He'd just happen to stop by the Trent law firm which was in the Maxwell town square across from the courthouse. The sun shone down brightly, and he thanked God for another gorgeous day.

Once Cyber Future's lawyers from the Jennings Law Firm got into town, things were really going to heat up. It wasn't every day that Maxwell saw a big trial. He wasn't a lawyer, but he heard that the only reason the trial was in Maxwell was because of some brilliant language in the contract no doubt crafted by lawyers at Hope's firm. The southern hospitality would only extend so far to those trying to take down one of the town's key businesses.

His first order of business today was keeping an eye on Hope. If Nola was operating his illegal businesses out of Maxwell, as Gabe thought he was, then his men were around the town, too. He'd been focused on the new people that had been coming through town lately. In fact, that's what first tipped him off to Nola's activities. Maxwell didn't get a lot of new residents. Yeah, a new family now and again wanting to get outside of Atlanta, but these were mostly single men employed at the Wakefield warehouse. And Gabe knew they were up to no good. What he hadn't been able to figure out yet is exactly what they were doing.

He strolled down to the town square and took a seat at one of the benches. He figured Hope would show up any minute.

He waited. And then he waited some more. What could be taking her so long? Just then he saw her. Dressed up in a fancy designer navy suit and high heels. Talk about a fish out of water.

He couldn't deny that she was beautiful. She had long blonde hair that she pulled back in a low ponytail the same as she wore in

New York. He'd noticed her big dark brown eyes too—a striking contrast to her hair. And thankfully, even though she was a city girl, she didn't go overboard with the makeup. Not that he was interested in her like that. They couldn't be more opposite.

She wasn't going to be happy to see him. A fact that became evident by the scowl that spread over her pretty face when she saw him sitting there on the bench.

She strode over to him with confident steps. "Agent Marino, you really have to stop stalking me."

"I'm not stalking you. And please don't call me Agent. I really don't think you want to interfere with an active FBI investigation."

"I'm not interfering. You're the one interfering with my life. You were probably the person trying to break into my hotel room last night at the inn. Just like you did in New York."

"Whoa. Wait a minute. What are you talking about?" He instantly jumped into full FBI mode.

"Someone tried to get into my room in the middle of the night."

"Did you call the police?"

"No." She took a step toward him. "It seemed silly. I thought it might've been you after all."

"I assure you, Hope. It wasn't me. You need to report it."

"Report what? They didn't actually get into my room. Maybe it was just a mix-up."

He took a deep breath. Was someone trying to hurt her? This new piece of information needed to be factored into his overall analysis of the Carlos Nola threat network. But why would Nola be going after Hope? That didn't exactly fit in his working theories. If not, Nola, then who?

"You need to be careful, Hope."

"Don't you find it funny that you're telling me that in this town? We're in the middle of nowhere Georgia. Doesn't exactly seem like the crime capital of the world."

"Small towns can be dangerous, too—unfortunately. Especially when there are criminal elements at work tied to powerful organized crime groups."

"Alleged criminal elements." She crossed her arms and frowned. "I have to get to work. Please let me do my job."

He nodded. "Sure. The Trent firm is just across the square."

"Thanks."

She walked away, and he figured he'd give her a little time while he worked some new angles and made some calls.

***

Hope couldn't get Gabe's deep southern drawl out of her head. He seemed sincere with those big brown eyes. She didn't really think it was him who had tried to get into her hotel room. Although if it wasn't him, she didn't want to think about the alternatives. She wanted to believe it was an accident, but she was going to be more cautious. What she needed to do was act like she was still in New York. She had to remind herself that she was still a woman alone in a strange town. No matter how cozy and quaint Maxwell seemed. She couldn't take her personal safety for granted.

She bit her bottom lip, concerned about connecting all the dots. Did what happened at the inn last night have anything to do with Gabe's investigation?

Trying to shake off an uneasy feeling, she looked up at the large house with white columns and big green ferns hanging from the porch. A sign hung from a large maple tree that said Trent Law Firm in sweeping dark print. Okay, she was totally not in New York anymore, she chuckled to herself.

She opened the front door slowly and walked in. Straight ahead of her was a woman with gray hair pulled up in a bun sitting at a desk with large frame maroon rimmed glasses.

"How may I help you?" She smiled widely.

"I'm Hope Finch. I'm from—"

"Oh, yes, yes, dear. I know who you are. We've been expecting you. Got you an office and everything all set up for you. I'm Patty, and I've worked here more years than you've been livin.'" The older woman laughed.

Hope couldn't help but grin. "Maxwell is a nice town."

"I know it's nothing like New York. I went to New York once to do Christmas shopping with my daughter. It was an experience that I'll never forget. I tell you though, my southern body can't handle that cold. Or all those people. It was like I was visiting another world. So I can only imagine how you feel here."

"I was born and raised there, so it's all I know."

"Once you get a taste of a smaller town, you'll fall in love. I can promise you that."

Hope highly doubted that she could come to love a way of life so different than her own. But she didn't want to be disrespectful so she didn't correct Patty's statement.

"Mr. Trent is waiting to see you. That's Trent senior or Greg as you probably know him. The junior Trent also works here, but he does real estate law mostly. Let me show you to his office first, and then you can get settled in before you go visit Wakefield Corporation."

Hope was impressed with Patty's introduction. Just because they were running a law firm on a much smaller scale, didn't mean that they weren't all highly professional and talented. They walked down a long hallway and into a large gorgeous office decorated with dark wood and navy hues. A big leather sofa occupied a portion and a mahogany desk sat by the window. An older man sat behind the desk with glasses on, reading a file.

"Greg, I've got Ms. Hope Finch here to see you."

Realizing he had company, Greg looked up and smiled at them both. "Thanks, Patty. I'll take good care of her."

Patty smiled and walked out of the room.

Greg walked out from behind his desk and outstretched his hand. "Hope, it's so good to finally meet you in person. After all those conference calls, I feel like I know you."

"It's nice to meet you, too. And thanks again for all your help with this case. I know Sam really appreciates it."

"He's scheduled to get in this week, too, right?"

"Yes, in a couple of days."

"I hope so. Trial starts on Monday." He laughed. "Have you ever been out to Wakefield Corp?"

"No. This is my first time in Maxwell. You know how it is. Nowadays we do so much work electronically. There hasn't been a need for me to travel here. Sam handled Lee's and Carlos's deposition. I think that was right before we got your firm involved."

"Yes. Well I'm glad you did. I don't trust those Cyber Future California attorneys from the Jennings Law Firm one bit. Someone has to keep their eye on them. I was reading through some of the emails, and I was appalled by some of the things they said. I get that not everyone is going to have our southern charm approach, but every lawyer should still comport themselves professionally. At least that's how I feel. I may be getting to be an old dinosaur, but it reflects badly on our profession when lawyers act like they do. It's no wonder we are the brunt of all the jokes."

"I think you're right. We had quite a bit of trouble with them during the extensive document exchange. They wrongfully withheld critical documents. And they're the plaintiff in the lawsuit." She shook her head remembering what a nightmare that was to deal with. Everything about Cyber Future was difficult. "We were going to move for sanctions against them, but in the end Sam decided it was better to focus on the merits and not the disputes over documents. They came up with some half-baked excuse that they accidentally kept documents in their possession because of a technical difficulty. We didn't want to push it."

"Sometimes we know what others are doing is wrong, and we have to make the best strategic decision to get the result our client wants in the least painful and most cost effective way." He paused. "Do you need a minute here or do you want to go ahead and make our way to Wakefield. I know Lee and his team are anxious to start the meetings."

"Oh, no. I'm fine to leave now." She walked toward the door. "This is such a beautiful office you have here."

"Thanks. As you could probably tell, it's an old house that we renovated. I just didn't have the heart to tear it down. So much history in this town dating back to the Civil War and beyond. Hopefully you'll get a little time to take some of that history in while you're here. There's a great tour around town, but it's only open during the summer. If you ever come back to visit, you'll definitely need to check it out. Bring your hand fan though because it gets hotter than ten skillets during the summer."

She was glad that they didn't tear down the old house. It really was amazing. As they walked back down the hall, she peeked into the other offices and saw they were also beautiful. For a split second, she wondered how different her life would be if she worked at a firm like this. Yes, Rice and Taylor was chic and modern. But there was something special about this old house that gave the Trent Firm added character. It was distinguished and homey at the same time. Homey was something she'd never experienced.

"I'll drive us over. It's just a few miles from here, and I can give you the quick tour of the town."

She stepped into his silver luxury sedan and there was no doubt in her mind that Greg Trent did really well for himself.

He turned the key to start the car. "Right now we're in the town square. Obviously, where our office is and the courthouse is just across the way."

"We're going to pass the Maxwell Inn, right?"

"Yes, we'll have to go past the inn and then a couple of miles further to our version of the suburbs. This block you see here is really our historic downtown area. Shops and a few restaurants. But the best eatin' in town is another block down."

"Yes, I actually went to Pa's last night."

"Great. Next you'll need to check out Mel's BBQ and also Billy's Shack."

She laughed. "All the restaurants have people's names in them."

He nodded. "That's just the way it works around here. They're named after the owners. All family owned and operated."

She looked out the window as they passed the inn and the restaurants. Then she could tell they were getting close to the suburbs, as Greg called it. Lots of big trees and grass. Even in the winter the grass still looked green to her. She loved all the trees and greenery. The area felt so vibrant and alive.

"Out here we got the big box stores and grocery. And lots of little neighborhoods. That's about it. Then we turn down this road coming up on the left and that's Wakefield Corporation. Both the corporate headquarters and the manufacturing facility is all out here."

She'd seen pictures of the company on the website, but she really wasn't prepared for what it looked like in person. In the middle of this Southern town stood a very large modern building. In direct opposition to the law firm and the inn. It was at least ten floors high and sprawling with a white high tech motif. "Wow," she said.

"Yeah, looks like a duck out of water, huh? Lee is from Maxwell, but he's a science geek through and through. He wanted the high tech feel to his company even if it sat in the heart of the Deep South. So that's exactly what he built. There's really nothing like it in any comparable southern town. One of a kind. Just like Lee himself."

"It looks even bigger than it does on the website."

"And it employs a lot of people. The entire customer service branch is stationed here. A huge chunk of the town works in that department. Then we have the tech people and engineers. The factory and warehouses are on site here, too, but further down the road. Wakefield owns all of this property. It's about fifty acres total, although a good portion of that is unused."

"It's amazing that Lee invented the Wakefield Chip. It really has revolutionized security applications for computers."

"Yeah. It's not as snazzy as those apps or whatever they call them. I'm not big into technology myself. I'm too old for that. But from what I understand it, most big companies are turning to the Wakefield Chip now. That's how this whole Cyber Future thing came about, right?"

"Yes. Cyber Future was one of our largest distributors of the Wakefield Chips. They're suing for breach of contract, but they're the ones who didn't hold up their end of the bargain. We—Wakefield—abided by the terms of the contract. They did not."

He nodded. "We will have to check in at the main desk. If you have any electronics those will have to be logged in by the receptionist."

"I have my laptop." Hope was even more impressed when she stepped into the reception area at Wakefield. Lush beige couches with ivory pillows were spread out in the lobby where a receptionist sat behind a white marble desk. A big chandelier hung down providing a bit of opulence. She could've been in Silicon Valley at a high tech company.

"Hi, Mary," Greg said to the receptionist.

"Good morning, Greg. And who do you have with you today?"

"This is Hope Finch. She's one of the lawyers from New York. We're here to see Lee and his group."

"Oh, yes." Mary was all business when Greg said the word Lee. She immediately picked up the phone and was only on the line for a moment. "They're ready to see you. Let me just get Ms. Finch's laptop serial number, and I'll have someone escort you up to the seventh floor."

Hope wasn't surprised about the security. Anytime you were dealing with technology and patents, companies were very wary. It didn't matter if you were their lawyer. Everyone followed the rules. No exceptions.

After the security check, a nice lady came around the corner to escort them up. A quick elevator ride to the seventh floor, and they were led to a large conference room.

"After you," Greg said.

Hope stepped into the room. Oh no. Not again. The conference room held a group of men. But there was one man sitting at the table who surely didn't belong. Special Agent Gabe Marino. He simply smiled at her. What game was this man playing?

The room had a large table fully equipped with technical equipment. A flat screen monitor hung on the wall. It was exactly what she would expect from a tech company.

She watched as Lee and Greg shook hands. She'd seen Lee's picture so she recognized the man. Tall, dark hair, and in his fifties. She also knew the other man in the room as the General Counsel at Wakefield--Will Cantwell who she had met before. Will wasn't a Maxwell native. Like her, he'd worked at a large New York law firm for years before taking the General Counsel position at Wakefield.

Introductions and handshakes were exchanged with Will and Lee. Then Gabe stood up and walked over to her.

"Hope," Lee said. "This is Gabe Marino. He lives here in Maxwell and does security consulting for us. I thought given the nature of this litigation, he should be involved."

Consulting, she thought. Did they not know what he did for a living either? How deep did his cover go? He made a slight head tick toward her. As if asking for her to keep quiet. Talk about dilemmas. Her gut told her that she shouldn't say anything until she understood the full circumstances of what was going on here. The last thing she wanted to do was to blow up an undercover FBI investigation.

"I know Sam is going to be taking the lead, but, Lee, I'd appreciate getting up to speed a bit," Greg said.

"Of course. I don't want to bore Hope with stuff she already knows. Gabe, why don't you show her around the facility and speak to her about some of the security issues we've discussed, so she's fully briefed on those concerns. Then we can regroup and talk trial logistics. We're at the less than a week countdown now."

This was actually good. She needed to talk to Gabe alone and figure out what was happening. "Thanks, Lee."

She walked out of the conference room with Gabe right behind her. She waited until they'd taken a few steps before she spoke. "You need to tell me what's going on right now."

"Wait just a second."

She could feel her temper starting to flare. Was Gabe playing all of them? Was his name even Gabe? Did he work for the FBI? The questions bubbled up as she waited for him to speak.

"Security consultant? Start talking," she demanded.

"Let me explain."

"I'm listening."

He looked around again making sure no one was around in the long corridor. "I told you the truth. I am working undercover as I explained to you. And my cover is as the owner of a security company that is based here in Maxwell. That's what people here believe I do."

"You realize how crazy this sounds? First, you show up in my apartment in New York with a highly questionable warrant. Then,

I travel down here and you appear out of thin air. And now, I have the CEO of my client under the impression that you're what? A security consultant?"

"I know it sounds suspect, and if I say you need to trust me, you'll probably laugh. But that's what I'm going to have to say."

She crossed her arms. "If you really suspected me of being involved with Nola's supposed criminal activities, then you wouldn't be telling me this."

"I had reason to think you might be involved, but after spending just a little time with you and doing some additional digging, I'm fairly certain you're not. I'm taking a risk, and hoping that you can help me. A literal leap of faith."

His eyes showed sincerity, but she questioned his entire story. "Who knows about you?"

"My cover is completely intact. I usually don't do much work in Maxwell. The only person in this town besides my mother that knows I'm FBI is the chief of police, Caleb Winters. It was too risky to expand beyond that. My security consulting company provides the perfect cover story for my travel and work schedule. Most people think when I leave to go to Atlanta each day that I'm actually out working jobs throughout the state. And then when I have to travel out of state, they assume I'm doing it for my security business. No one has ever questioned it. I've been doing it like this for five years. It also serves as a solid cover for work I need to do for the FBI elsewhere. So it's something that needs to stay in place."

"You've got it all figured out, huh?"

He shook his head. "Far from it where this case is concerned. I literally fell into this investigation."

"I have a hard time believing that. What does that even mean for an FBI agent? Aren't you assigned your cases anyway?"

"Usually, I am assigned cases. But sometimes we find cases ourselves and bring them in. Given our line of work, you never know what you're going to be exposed to. Where your sources take you."

"And how did that play out in this case?"

"There's been an uptick in crime in Maxwell. I started snooping around and the facts didn't add up to me. Counterfeiting, drugs, a couple of muggings. Yeah, we have small town crime, but the counterfeiting really troubled me. Add to that picture an influx of new residents that don't really fit in, and I knew something was going on. I did some intelligence gathering and every road leads back to Nola. And to Wakefield. Bank accounts, shell companies. I believe that Nola has set up illegal businesses throughout the south. I think he's expanding his operation into Maxwell and using Wakefield Corporation to help cover his tracks."

"So now you've convinced Lee that Wakefield needs a security consultant so you can have access to conduct your FBI investigation."

He nodded. "Basically. So you can see why I need you to stay quiet. But beyond that, I'm still going to need your help."

"My help." She shook her head. "My help? I'm about to start a major trial in less than a week. How in the world can I help you with this half-baked investigation?"

"Just give me a chance. If you want to do the right thing, then you know that as their lawyer you need to protect Wakefield's interests. Just think of the company's exposure because of Nola's activities. That alone should cause you to want to assist the FBI. That's in addition to just being a good citizen, and a steward of the law."

"And how exactly do you plan to get proof that will hold up in court against Nola? Assuming that any such proof exists?"

"I told you I needed your help, and I meant it."

"What exactly does that mean?"

"We're a team. I know you have work to do so that you can prepare for trial, but you also have access. You've got eyes and ears in places I don't."

"I'm not a spy. I'm an attorney." She stood with her hands on her hips trying to give off an air of defiance. He wasn't budging though. Yeah, he might have the inside track to Lee, but he had no in with Nola. But Nola was not only a witness at trial, he was her witness. She was responsible for getting him ready to testify. This could go sideways really fast if she didn't rein Gabe in.

"I know exactly what you are. And I'm not asking you to be something you're not. That's the beauty of this investigation. You simply have to be you."

"And you get around the attorney client privilege how?"

"I'm a consultant for Wakefield Corporation."

"Under false pretenses."

"But the more important piece is something you're very aware of. Nola is not your client."

She sighed. "Show me around while I think about this." She needed time to gather her thoughts. To implement a plan. He was right about Nola. Her loyalty was to Wakefield Corporation, not to Nola as an individual man.

"Sure. You need to know your way around here anyway."

She only half listened as he talked about the different floors in the main headquarters. After a few minutes, she tried to shake herself out of the foggy haze. She needed to be on her game right now.

"Let's go outside, and I'll show you where the factory is," he said. Then he looked at her again. "Are you okay to walk with those heels you've got on?"

"Don't worry about me."

They took the elevator down to the first floor and walked outside. The sun was shining brightly today, and she was glad she hadn't worn a jacket on top of her suit.

She took a moment and looked at him again. His dark hair was neatly styled and instead of a suit he wore a long sleeved button down and khakis. He definitely stood over six feet tall.

"This way."

She jumped when he put his hand on her back guiding her down a long sidewalk. She was on edge. She didn't think she was in any danger from this man. But she was definitely going to do some research to make sure he actually was an FBI agent.

"When are you meeting with Nola?" he asked.

"Tomorrow. At Greg's firm. We've done a lot of preparation work over the phone, but there's no substitute for a face to face meeting when you're talking about trial testimony."

They walked in silence down a long sidewalk until the area became more wooded. Trees and shrubbery shaded the path blocking out most of the sunlight. She felt like she was headed into the middle of a campsite. "How do the plant workers get back here?" She eyed the narrow path skeptically.

"There's a totally separate entrance. When you make the turn into the main headquarters, if you keep going and take a left it will bring you all the way on the other side of the plant. We're basically coming at it from the back. So this path isn't used all that often, but it's here if needed."

A shiver shot down her arm as she glanced around. Feeling like someone was watching them. She turned around and surveyed the area. She didn't see anyone, but the feeling was strongly there. The thick tree branches swayed back and forth in the light breeze.

He stopped and turned toward her. "You okay?" he asked.

"Yeah. There's something just a bit creepy about being back here. We went from total sunlight on a mild winter's day to dark woods in about five minutes."

"We can turn back, and I can take you by car around the other side if you'd like."

"No. We've made it this far. It's not like anything is going to happen to us." She heard the words and realized she was actually trying to convince herself. This was not a normal case. And someone had tried to break into her room last night. What if Gabe was right and she had somehow gotten herself involved in the middle of something dangerous? Could she even trust Gabe? There was someone in those woods, she just knew it. But her eyes told her otherwise.

She realized that they were both staring at each other and had come to a standstill. She broke away and kept walking. He was right there beside her.

Eager to focus on the task at hand she started talking. "So what do you want me to do with Nola tomorrow?"

"I need you to be careful. Yes, I want your help, but if you go in asking too many questions that may not seem relevant, then Nola might get suspicious. I don't want to worry you, but it could be that Nola is already checking you out. Making sure that you won't cause him any problems. You need to stay on his good side no matter what. There is too much risk involved if we play it any other way."

She let his words sink in as they walked in silence the rest of the way to the plant. There was not only a lot she didn't know about Nola, but there was also a lot she didn't know about Gabe. Yeah, he said he was an FBI agent, which she tended to believe. But who was the real Gabe Marino?

***

As Gabe looked in Hope's eyes, he saw a flicker of fear. She wouldn't admit it, of course, but he'd dropped a lot of information on her. Being a very smart woman, she wouldn't just take him at face value. But he'd seen those wheels turning. She was strategizing, and that was fine with him.

He wanted her to act smart. He'd taken a big risk in trusting her to keep his cover intact. And now he needed her to play a role with Nola. One that only she could play, and one that was absolutely vital to his investigation. If he was going to crack this case, he needed hard evidence against Nola. There was simply no other way.

His access to Wakefield Corporation had helped convince him that Lee was on the up and up. But Lee had no idea what Nola was doing right under his nose. He needed to gather the evidence to prove it. Assertions and innuendo wouldn't fly in court and they wouldn't be enough to take to Lee.

"So this is the manufacturing plant," Hope said. She stood looking up at the large industrial facility.

"This is it. Plus all the warehouses." He pointed toward his right. "I think Nola may be using some of the facilities for his drug business."

"How is it possible to do that in plain sight?"

"He'd need help from some of the plant workers, but there is plenty of room to hide narcotics. I told you there were some new men in town over the past six to nine months. Well they all work here. Don't you find that just a bit suspicious?"

She nodded. "It sounds like it's worth looking into."

"I may need you to come out here with me again at night when we can do some reconnaissance."

"Why don't I like the sound of that?" She quirked an eyebrow.

He didn't want to say too much right now. "We need to get back to Lee and Greg. We've been gone long enough for them to have caught Greg up on everything."

"All right. Let's head back." She didn't wait for him to answer and started walking.

Hope definitely had a mind of her own. But that might come in handy for his purposes. A strong willed woman like Hope would be what was needed to get information from Nola.

When they walked back into the executive conference room, Lee, Greg, and Will were sitting around the table drinking coffee.

"Great timing," Lee said. "We're ready to talk about scheduling for trial prep, Hope."

"Wonderful." She smiled and took a seat at the table. "Sam arrives in two days. He'll meet with you when he gets here. I think he wants two full days of preparation time with you Lee. And Will, you should also be in those meetings. I've got responsibility for preparing Carlos. You two are our main affirmative witnesses. Sam and I are also working on cross-examination for the Cyber Future guys. Those are pretty much good to go. And then Sam will adapt on the fly to whatever the direct examination brings."

"I want all the preparation time I can get," Lee said. "I'm willing to sit and prepare all day every day until trial starts. This lawsuit is frivolous. If anything, we're the wronged party here."

"You know that Sam and I will do whatever it takes to make sure you and all of our witnesses are completely comfortable."

"Since you'll be working with Carlos one-on-one, just a warning that he isn't the most patient man. But he's brilliant. He understands what this lawsuit means to the company, and he assured me he would take it all very seriously."

"Oh, on our telephone calls, he's been very focused. I think he understands how important this litigation is to the company. And he wants Wakefield to thrive."

"Perfect. I think that's it for now."

"I'll go back to Greg's office and start getting settled in." Hope stood up and walked quickly out of the room.

Now it was just him and the other men.

"Make sure you keep your eyes open, Gabe," Lee said. "I just have a feeling that this entire trial could get ugly. And I don't trust a single one of those people from Cyber Future. Or their lawyers. I need you to be my eyes and ears. Got it?"

"Yes, sir." If Lee had a bad feeling now, Gabe hated to think what he'd feel if he knew all the facts. Another reason he needed something concrete on Nola. Sooner rather than later.

CHAPTER FOUR

"You shouldn't be here," Hope said. She tried to organize the files that had been shipped down from New York onto her temporary desk at the Trent Law Firm.

Gabe took a few steps into her office. "Actually, you heard Lee. He wants me to be very involved."

"That doesn't mean crowding me when I'm actually trying to work. Believe it or not, this trial is happening, and I have to prepare."

"You need to be focused on Nola."

She looked up into his serious eyes. Was this guy really trying to tell her what to do? And how to do her job? No way. "Look, I told you I would try to help you. But what I will not allow is you bossing me around. You're not a partner in my law firm. I don't work for you. I'm still trying to figure out exactly what you are, but right now you seem more like a rogue FBI agent to me."

"Keep your voice down." He stepped closer to her. "My cover has to stay intact, or this operation will never work."

"Do you want to try the case for me, too? Maybe you can step in and replace Sam as first chair." She tried to keep her temper from flaring, but she wasn't doing a great job.

"No need to get upset. We need to work as a team, remember?"

She huffed. "Teammates don't tell each other what to do. They work together. They listen to each other. Respect each other."

"All right. Let me start over then. I'd really like you to focus on the Nola interview tomorrow. What would you like to work on?"

She couldn't help but smile when he gave a bit of a goofy grin. She quickly reminded herself that she was mad at him. But in the end, she was a legal professional. "I also plan on preparing for the interview. I was just trying to get my files in order first."

"Hello there. Sorry to interrupt."

Hope looked toward the door and Patty was standing there.

"I'm about to leave for the evening. Do you two need anything from me before I do?"

"No, Patty. We're good here," she said.

Patty nodded. "Greg asked me to apologize to you. He has an event at the country club tonight that he can't miss. But he said that Gabe had volunteered to make sure you're well taken care of tonight. We can't have you all alone out in Maxwell not knowing anyone or where to eat and all of that."

Of course he did, she thought. She wasn't going to say anything to Patty though. "Thank you, Patty. We're good here."

"Gabe knows how to lock up."

Patty walked out, leaving them alone.

"You have keys to the law firm?" she asked.

"I am a security consultant. These people know me and trust me." He paused. "And more importantly I'd just done a security consult for the firm. So I know all the ends and outs of their security system."

"Still you're pretending to be something you're not." She tried to wrap her head around his ruse. She knew it was required for his job, but she didn't know he lived like that.

"I think we just started our relationship on the wrong foot."

"We don't have a relationship, Agent Marino."

"Business relationship. Waiting for you inside your apartment in New York and presenting you with the search warrant probably wasn't the best move."

"And?"

"I'm sorry for that, but I felt it was important to meet you. Here we are now and there are a lot of issues going on. Obviously the first and most pressing being your meeting with Carlos Nola tomorrow."

"Why don't you check to make sure no one else is in the office before we start talking," she asked quietly.

He nodded and walked out of her office. She took a deep breath trying to compose herself. There was something about Gabe that threw her off kilter just a tad. Small, but enough to be disconcerting. She'd allowed herself to get spooked today while walking those trails in between the facilities. And then there was the incident in her room at the inn. It was all coming together and starting to make her paranoid. There was no reason for her to be afraid of anything. At this point, all Gabe had was loose speculation. No concrete evidence. Not even close. Nor did she have any particular reason to fear for her own personal safety.

"We're all clear. Everyone has gone home for the night. Why don't we try to get a game plan together and then get you out here? I know you must be hungry after the light lunch at Wakefield."

Instead of directly responding, she sat down at the desk and opened up her file. He took a seat across from her.

"You need to understand, that I have a duty to prepare Nola for his examination on the witness stand. That duty doesn't change because of your investigation. It's something I take very seriously. Something that I've worked years at to be able to do in court."

He leaned back in his chair. "I'm not asking you to shirk you responsibilities with Nola. But if the opportunities arise to get information that could be helpful, then you should take it. Only if it doesn't seem like you're prying into something that has no relevance to the lawsuit or your understanding of the how the company works."

"I get that you're worried about it being obvious, but I think I can handle myself. Carlos and I have talked numerous times on the phone plus I've met him in person. Each time we had a positive and helpful conversation. He'd have absolutely no reason to think that I was in any way a threat to him."

"Let's keep it that way."

"I can't operate in the dark. I need more specifics on what you actually have on him."

Gabe looked down and then back up. "Specifics might be a bit too strong of a characterization."

She laughed. "Basically you have no evidence—just theories. Correct?"

"Correct, counselor." He leaned forward in his chair. "But as you know, it all starts with a theory."

"And what you've told me so far is that there's been an increase in crime here, some new residents that have raised your suspicions."

"Right. Plus the tangible evidence we do have is the existence of shell companies, or what I believe to be shell companies, routed under Wakefield that are really just Nola's businesses."

"Isn't that easy enough to check out and verify?"

Gabe shook his head. "It's not as easy as you would think. On paper everything looks solid."

"Which is why there is no evidence."

"Exactly. The company's paperwork may be totally legitimate. But that doesn't mean the company is operating a legal business. Nola has associates throughout the southeast, working for him. Drug running, money laundering, you name it."

"Or, he could be operating totally above board companies." She walked around the desk and sat on the corner. Her mind raced. "Why here? And why Wakefield?"

"Nola approached Lee about six years ago about becoming a board member. He has a house in Atlanta, and was looking to expand his local business ties. Nola didn't jump in immediately. That's not his MO. He does the work, gains the trust, and then when the time is right he makes the shift."

"That's strategic."

"Yeah. And Wakefield is a great target. A large company that also has manufacturing facilities in a small town."

"But you feel like Nola is the only dirty one in the bunch at Wakefield?"

"Yes. I've found nothing indicating that anyone else in management or on the board is involved. All the more reason you should want to help put this guy away. He's harming your client. And exposing them to liability. Just think about the lawsuits that could follow if I'm right."

"I never said I didn't want to help. Just that I wanted to understand the allegations and what the real state of play was here. I have obligations to Wakefield Corporation as their counsel. Those have to be front and center for me. You have obligations to the FBI. From what I'm hearing, I think those interests align." She paused. "At least for now anyway."

"So tomorrow as you're preparing Nola just use your best judgment. You get what we're trying to do here."

"Yeah." She felt a shiver go down her arm. Lawyering was one thing, but this whole undercover angle was making her a bit nervous.

"You ready to get out of here?"

"One more thing. What do you know about Cyber Future?"

He cocked his head to the side. "You know, I haven't done much recon on them at all. Why do you ask?"

"Their lawyers at the Jennings Law Firm are a dirty bunch. The most ethically questionable lawyers I've dealt with in the five years I've been practicing law. Wouldn't surprise me if there wasn't something illegal going on with them. I'm not saying it has anything to do with Nola, or is anything like you suspect him of. Probably more along the lines of tax evasion or something." She sighed. "This is rampant speculation on my part, or maybe wishful thinking because their lawyers have been so difficult to deal with."

"Just because lawyers are shifty doesn't mean there's anything going on with the company. But we can keep our eyes on them, too."

"Good." She smiled. "Now lock up and let's go to dinner. I'm starving."

***

Hope Finch was a complicated woman. Gabe felt like he was only beginning to scratch the service where she was concerned. He had to remind himself when she looked at him with those big innocent brown eyes that she was off limits. For a multitude of reasons. Just because she was smart and attractive, that wouldn't do it. He'd been told by his family about a million times that he was too picky. And that at thirty years old, he needed to start thinking about settling down. The thing was, every woman he had ever dated had disappointed him.

His last girlfriend had been pretty and sweet. A strong woman of faith. But she didn't understand his job. She couldn't comprehend how much he loved it and how much time it took. A reoccurring theme with his relationships with having to keep up his cover as a security consultant.

He wasn't willing to quit the FBI for any woman. That would never happen. His job was his focus and he was driven to move up the chain at the FBI. He would love to be running the Atlanta field office one day. He kept praying that God would send the right woman his way. And he'd be patient and wait until that day came. For now he had a bad guy to put away.

He also had to make sure that he didn't put Hope into a situation she couldn't handle. Like she said, she was a lawyer. Not an

FBI agent. She hadn't been trained like he had. The thought of her being in danger twisted his gut. But she had the best opportunity to get him the information and evidence he needed.

"What's for dinner?"

Her question broke him out of his thoughts as they walked down the sidewalk.

"It's time for some Maxwell barbeque. You up for it, city girl?"

She laughed. "I have had barbeque before, you know."

He opened the car door for her. "But you've never had our barbeque in Maxwell. Mel's is famous for the best BBQ in the state. Some say best in the south."

"You're really setting the bar high."

As he cranked up the car, he couldn't help but grin. "I'm telling you, you may be so full, I'll have to carry you out of there."

"I highly doubt that."

He watched as she fidgeted with her suit jacket. "What's wrong?"

"Can we stop by the inn first so I can change clothes? I'm really tired of wearing this suit."

"I thought you big fancy New York lawyers practically slept in your designer suits. Isn't that a way of life up there?"

She laughed loudly. "When I'm not at work I'm a jeans and t-shirt kind of girl."

"I would've never guessed that."

"You sure do have a lot of preconceived notions about me just because I'm from New York. It's not very nice to prejudge, you know."

"I bet most of them are accurate." He glanced over at her and watched as she scowled.

She huffed. "I highly doubt that."

"We'll just have to see."

It only took them a minute to get to the inn.

"I'll just run in and change. It will only take me a minute and be back before you know it."

"I've heard that line before."

"Believe it or not, I'm not a high maintenance woman."

Looking at how put together she looked, he found that hard to believe.

She stepped out of the car and walked toward the inn. He rubbed his temples. It had been a long day and the next week was only going to get a lot longer. True to her word about five minutes later, she walked back to the car. She wore a green sweater and jeans. But she was frowning.

"What's wrong?" he asked.

She sat in silence for a moment, and he didn't move the car. He had to hear what was bothering her.

"My room," she finally said. "Something felt off. Like someone had been in there."

"Well I'm sure the cleaning staff was in there."

"No, not like that. I had one file that I'd carried with me on the plane. I didn't take it with me today, and it seemed like the papers had been shifted. Nothing obvious. But I think I remember exactly how I had that file and it doesn't look the same way now."

"I don't want to downplay your concerns, but do you think all I've shared is just making you a little paranoid? Was there anything of special note in the file?"

"No. Or at least it didn't hold special significance to me. It was information about Wakefield, but Nola would already have access to it."

"Wait a minute." He started the car and pulled out of the hotel on the way to the restaurant. "What if it had nothing to do with Nola? What if it was connected to the litigation?"

"You think it was Cyber Future?"

"You said they were unscrupulous."

She sighed loudly. "But breaking and entering is taking it a bit further than shady lawyering, don't you think?"

"It's probably nothing, but it's something to keep in mind. You need to be careful." As soon as he turned right onto the street, he saw the headlights come up quickly behind him. Too quickly.

Hope must have sensed something was wrong because she turned around. "What are they doing? I thought this was a friendly small southern town? Not angry big city road ragers."

"Something's wrong. No one around here would act like that. Hold on tight." His first mission was to protect Hope. Yes, he had an investigation to carry out, but he was a federal agent with an innocent civilian in his care. He couldn't allow her to be harmed.

He pressed the gas hard, keeping a firm grip on the wheel. But the truck kept up the tail.

"He's gaining on us, Gabe."

He didn't want to drive out of the city, but there wasn't much way to lose the guy in the middle of town. What did the guy in the truck want? Whatever it was, it wasn't good.

He eyed his rearview mirror. The truck was speeding up as the bright lights sped closer to his car. At any moment, the truck could ram them. Making a split second decision, he took a hard right onto a small side street skidding up onto the sidewalk with a jolt. The truck flew right by them.

"Whoa," Hope said. Then silence filled the car. Neither of them said a word for a moment.

He realized he was holding his breath. Letting out the air, his heart pounded.

"That wasn't random was it?" she asked.

"I don't think so." He took a deep breath and looked over at her. "Are you all right?"

"Yes, I'm fine. You think that was Cyber Future, too?"

"I'm not sure. Hope, is there a reason they would target you beyond you just being a lawyer for Wakefield?"

She shook her head. "I don't think so. My mind is swimming right now. But when we were on the trail at Wakefield, I felt like someone was out there. Watching us."

"Why didn't you say something at the time?"

"I didn't want you to think I was crazy. I thought maybe I was just a bit on edge after what happened at the inn."

He reached out and touched her shoulder. "We need to figure this out. Someone might be targeting you."

***

The next morning Hope's hands shook as she tried to clasp her silver necklace together behind her neck. Target. The word replayed in her head. Last night weighed heavily on her. She was certain someone had been in her room going through her stuff, and after the truck incident she was even more convinced. There was no way these were random or isolated events. Every instinct she had was telling her something was terribly wrong.

The barbeque dinner turned out to be a pretty somber experience. The food had been good, but she could barely taste it because of her stomach churning. And now her stomach churned again, but for a different reason. She was about to have her meeting with Carlos Nola.

How quickly things could change. She thought that she had a good relationship with Nola, and was comfortable around him and talking to him. They'd made solid progress on trial preparation. Before she'd come to Maxwell, she'd mapped out exactly what they would need to go over in their meeting. But now she started to question it all.

She somehow had to get it together. She had a trial to prepare for. And until she had some more solid evidence against Nola, she couldn't shirk her obligations. Wakefield Corporation had hired her firm to defend them in the lawsuit, and that's exactly what she had to do. To be able to put on a proper defense, Nola had to be a strong witness. She intended to prepare him to be just that. Whatever personal issues she was having would just have to be secondary.

As she walked out of the inn toward the Trent Law firm, she shivered even though she wasn't cold. "Get a grip," she muttered. It was broad daylight, almost nine a.m. She couldn't allow herself to be more nervous about the short walk to the town square than walking alone in New York at night. Something she did every single night in fact. She was being ridiculous.

A slight breeze blew her hair back from her face. She'd worn it down today instead of her usual low ponytail. Humming a song, she instantly started to relax as the breeze picked up. It was a gorgeous sunny day, and Hope could easily tell why the Maxwell winter weather would be a huge draw for its residents.

As she took a step around the corner, a strong hand grabbed her arm and pulled her toward him. She felt something sharp jab into her ribs.

"Don't scream if you want to live." The man's voice was deep and evil in her ear.

Her entire body shook as her heart screamed in fear. She was going to die. Right there on a side street in the middle of Maxwell, Georgia. Death was staring her in the face.

Looking up all she could see was a pair of dark eyes. The tall man wore his cap very low and a big scarf around his neck and lower face. A scarf much too heavy for the mild winter day.

"Where is the chip?" he asked. He pushed her up against the building blocking her way.

"What chip?"

He looked around quickly then thrust his forearm into her throat cutting off her air supply. "I'm not playing games. Tell me where it is now."

She could barely draw a breath. She tried to shake her head no. He loosened his grip a little.

"I promise you, I have no idea what chip you are talking about."

"The Cyber Future Chip that Wakefield stole," he growled. "Where is it?"

Stars appeared before her eyes and she got dizzy. Her body was about to give way.

"Now," he yelled.

His eyes were lit up and showing pure evil. Would God protect her now?

"I don't know. I don't know," she whispered. He pushed his arm harder into her throat.

"Hope!" Gabe's voice rang out.

"We're not done here." The man took a step back, freeing her from his awful grip. He ran away down the street.

She felt like she was going to collapse, but then Gabe was there with her. His arms holding her up.

"Are you all right? What just happened?" he asked.

She looked up into his dark eyes—so unlike those of the man who had attacked her. "That man." She paused, trying to take a breath. "He grabbed me. I never saw him coming."

"Did he steal something from you?"

Taking a few deep breaths she steadied herself. "No, Gabe. That wasn't a mugger. He knew who I was."

Gabe narrowed his eyes and dropped his hands from her arms, now that she was steady. "What do you mean?"

"He told me to give him the chip." It was still difficult to get enough air. "I asked him what he was talking about. He definitely thought I had something."

"What chip?"

"That was my question. He claims that Wakefield stole a chip from Cyber Future."

"Wow." Gabe ran his hand through his hair.

"But I've got to get to the office. Nola is probably already there waiting for me."

"Are you sure you're up for this now?"

"I have to be."

Gabe looked down at her. "Your neck is red. He hurt you."

"I'll be fine." As she said the words, even she could hear that they were stated without much conviction. But she couldn't just roll over. She had to figure out what was going on. What was her attacker talking about? The man who might have the answers was the one she was due to meet. And she was definitely going to ask.

"Could you identify the man?"

She shook her head. "Probably not. All I got a good look at were his eyes. His scarf and hat obstructed his face. That wasn't coincidental."

"Nola has to be involved in this alleged theft."

"If there's any truth to it, then that's a distinct possibility. I'm going to ask him."

"Just straight out?"

"He'll probably wonder why my neck looks like this. I need to gauge what he knows. We may have bigger problems than Nola's crime ring in Maxwell." She turned around and started walking toward the office. She hated being late.

He grabbed her arm. "Are you absolutely sure you can handle this right now? You just got accosted in the middle of the street."

She shifted back around to face him. "Yes. More than ever I need answers. If someone thinks I know something I don't know or have something I don't have, then I could be in real danger. This is only the beginning."

"I'm coming with you." He started walking to keep up with her pace.

"You know you can't come into the meeting. A general meeting at Wakefield is one thing, but this is different."

"I won't go in. I just want to make sure you get there okay."

She relented. It actually made her feel a bit better with him by her side.

"That was a pretty gutsy move approaching you on the street."

"He had something jabbed into my side." She touched her side and knew she would be bruised. "I don't know whether it was a knife or a gun. But to a passerby until he put his forearm on my throat, no one would've noticed anything was awry."

"And you're sure you don't know what he's talking about?"

"No. Wakefield is in the business of making all types of chips and technology. Why would they need to steal something from Cyber Future? Wakefield is cutting edge."

"Unless Cyber Future has something better and more lucrative. Wakefield found out about it."

"Hmm…" Her mind raced with possibilities. "What if someone at Wakefield figured out that Cyber Future had some type of special technology during its review of the documents for this case?" She asked more to herself than to Gabe.

"That might explain why Cyber Future was sending someone after you. But for him to threaten you like that, this has to be huge. Not just a random computer chip filled with routine technology."

This was the last thing she needed before trial. "All right. I'll talk to you when this meeting is over."

"Why don't I meet you back here at the firm? I don't feel comfortable with you going around alone right now until we have a better understanding of the threat level."

The words threat level sent another chill down her arm. She didn't argue. Instead she took a deep breath and walked into the law firm. Carlos Nola was sitting in the reception area with a cup of coffee and the Maxwell newspaper.

"Mr. Nola, I'm so sorry I'm late."

"No problem," he said. "And you know to call me Carlos." Then he set down his paper and looked up at her. His eyes widened. "Hope, what happened to you?"

"I'd rather discuss it in my office."

"Certainly." He allowed her to lead the way to the office she was using.

"Please sit down and I'll explain."

Her neck must have looked even worse than she imagined for him to be staring at her with his big, wide green eyes.

"Do you need to see a doctor?"

"I'll be fine." It seemed like he was truly concerned about her. Was he really the criminal mastermind that Gabe had alleged?

"Please tell me what happened."

"I was attacked on the way to the office this morning."

"Oh no."

"But that's really not the headline, Mr. Nola."

He raised a curious eyebrow.

"My attacker wanted me to tell him where the chip was."

"What?" Nola leaned forward.

"Do you know anything about Wakefield stealing some sort of chip from Cyber Future?"

Nola blew out a breath looking down and back up. "No. That's a serious allegation."

"With all due respect, Mr. Nola, I felt firsthand how serious it was." She was walking a line, but given what had just happened to her she felt she was more than justified.

He shook his head "I'm so sorry, Hope. Of course. I can't even imagine what you must be feeling right now."

"So back to my question. Mr. Nola, I need you to be completely forthright with me. Do you know anything about this? Anything at all?"

He looked her straight in the eye and didn't waver. "No. I'm sorry, but I don't."

He seemed truthful, but she couldn't accept him at face value. Not given all the events.

"I'll need to inform Lee about what happened. Regardless he needs to know that one of his lawyers was attacked, and that

Cyber Future may be making serious allegations of theft and be willing to engage in retaliation."

"How does this impact the trial?"

"It doesn't. Our lawsuit is a fairly straightforward breach of the supply contract. Yes, the dollar amount is quite large, but they haven't made any allegations of theft in the suit and it's too late now for this trial. And regardless the fact that a man attacked me makes me think this might be something they want to fly under the radar as opposed to working within the legal system."

"I've never trusted those guys. From day one, I was the one warning Lee that we needed to stay away from them. But they were offering the most favorable contract terms." Nola stood up and started pacing back and forth. "We're missing something here about why anyone would be interested in hurting you."

"I fear there's a lot we're missing."

"Beyond the obvious. Cyber Future is planning something. I can feel it."

"Then we need to determine what that is ASAP."

"We should loop Lee in. He also hired a security consultant. We should make sure the consultant's involved too."

Well wasn't that the perfect way for Gabe to get access. "I agree. But we need to do a little preparation for the trial. Then I'll call Sam and let him know what's going on and we can meet with the others."

"All right. But you should start considering that we've got a lot bigger things to worry about than this lawsuit."

CHAPTER FIVE

G abe watched as Hope stepped out of the firm and looked around. She was on edge—it showed in her body language as she fidgeted with her hair and suit jacket. What had happened in there with Nola?

Gabe prayed for guidance. Who was the bigger threat? Cyber Future or Nola? The immediate answer appeared to be Cyber Future. Just the thought of that man with his hands on Hope, hurting her, angered him. And in his town. Things like this didn't happen in Maxwell, or at least they shouldn't be happening. But he felt like he was thinking that way too much lately.

"Hope." He walked up toward her. The visible relief on her face as her shoulders relaxed made him feel good. The last thing he wanted was to add to her stress.

"Looks like you're going to get what you want. We're going for a ride."

"What do you mean?" They started walking toward his car.

"Nola wants the security consultant, meaning you, to be involved in this Cyber Future investigation that he's launching. He just got off the phone with Lee. They want a meeting at Wakefield to discuss our response. I just looped Sam Upton in. He's my boss and the partner on the litigation."

He turned the key in the ignition and wondered how this would play out. "Nola has heard about me?"

"Yes, from Lee. I guess that Lee has been impressed with your work so far." She looked at him. "What exactly have you done?"

"A full security assessment of the main building. My next move is for the warehouses which is where I really wanted to go."

"Whatever is it, you're on Lee's good side for sure."

"I take it that Nola denied knowing anything about the chip?"

She sighed and leaned her head back on the headrest. "Yes. And the thing was, he looked so believable. But I know better than to just trust him. Regardless, he seemed really concerned about my welfare."

"What now?" he asked.

"A group meeting at Wakefield. They also called in the chief of police and his deputy."

This was getting way bigger than his initial investigation. He would have to report in to his boss soon. These new developments made his job harder but provided him even more access to Wakefield and Nola.

He felt his fingers clench on the wheel. "We need a plan."

"There isn't much we can do at this initial meeting beyond explaining what happened and trying to discover more information. How will the police chief be with you?"

"He's totally solid and you can trust him with your life. He's pretty young for a police chief. We grew up together. His name is Caleb Winters. We won't have any issue with him. The deputy chief on the other hand is a different story. His name is Mike Ramsey. He's twenty years Caleb's senior. Has a big chip on his shoulder about not being the chief."

"Why isn't he?"

"He's lived in Maxwell long enough to make more enemies than friends. In his earlier years on the force, he was known to look the other way for some folks and real close at others."

"And what are you going to offer Lee in terms of the assistance you can provide him?"

"Whatever he wants. But the biggest thing is I'm going to ask for full access. Given the threat from Cyber Future, he'll probably grant it. I want to be able to come and go as I please and have full security clearances into the building and its facilities."

"And Caleb will guard your cover?"

"Absolutely. He's former Special Forces. He will not give up an FBI agent."

"Good. Now I'm trying to figure out how I need to handle this, too. Sam totally flipped out when I called him. He's dropping everything and flying in tonight. I could barely have a rational conversation with him on the phone he was so amped up about the whole thing. He even threatened to send me home."

"What?"

"Yes. He's worried about my own personal security. And he's a good guy, I have no doubt he's worried. But he's also concerned about one of the attorneys at his firm being attacked. I'm sure he's thinking liability and exposure. He's a litigator. He'd be crazy not to. I know how these guys think."

Would it be safer to send Hope back to New York? The hired guns for Cyber Future could find her anywhere. No, she was safer in Maxwell in a contained environment where he could protect her. He patted his gun in his holster almost subconsciously in response. "Here we are. You ready?"

She didn't look ready. Her normally rosy cheeks were pale and her eyes narrowed. "I guess so." She looked out the window. "Looks like the police are already here."

He reached over and grabbed her hand, squeezing tight. "We're going to get through this, Hope. I promise you that. I'm not going to let anything happen to you. Now that I know you're a target, I'm not letting you out of my sight."

He felt her shiver a bit under his touch. Maybe he shouldn't have used the word target, even if it was the truth.

"I'm good. It's just been a lot to deal with. My mind was set on being second chair at this trial and what a huge opportunity it was for my career advancement. Moving up the ladder at the firm. Then ever since you showed up in my apartment, my life has been topsy turvy." She paused. "I'm not blaming you. I'm just saying everything has been crazy since then." She pulled her hand away from his and opened the car door.

No doubt that Hope Finch was a complex woman. And then some. Wasn't she the type of woman that would challenge him? That would understand about his career? No. He couldn't think that way right now. His first duty as a federal agent was to this investigation, and as part of that, to make sure no innocent civilians—including Hope—were harmed.

The conference room was buzzing with excitement, but not the good kind. The kind that gripped your nerves and led you to the brink. Lee's face was visibly red.

"So glad you're here, Gabe." Lee shook his hand. Then Lee strode over to Hope and grabbed her hands. "Are you okay? What kind of monster would attack a young woman?"

Before Hope could even respond Lee kept on talking. "Hope, I take that attack on you as an attack on all of us. Please know that I'm not going to spare any expense in tracking down this man. He threatened you personally, and he threatened our company."

"Thank you, Lee."

"Let's everyone gather around the table and have a seat so we can discuss this pressing matter."

Gabe took note of the people in the room. For Wakefield it was Lee, Nola, and Will the general counsel. Caleb and his deputy chief Mike both wore grim faces showing little expression. Hope's color still hadn't returned to her cheeks.

"First things first," Lee said. "I want to hear Hope's story first hand with no interrupting. That way this group all has the benefit of hearing it from her and not from someone retelling it. You know how that can be." Lee paused taking a sip of coffee. "Hope, the floor is yours."

Even though she was certainly nervous and probably still justifiably afraid, he watched as she composed herself before she spoke. Hope's strength was a quality that not everyone had. And it seemed to come from an authentic place. He no longer thought that she could be involved in anything illegal with Nola.

"Maybe I should back up before I talk about what happened this morning, I think it would be useful for everyone to hear what else has occurred since I've gotten into town."

"What do you mean?" Lee interjected. "There's more?"

"I think if you let Hope explain, it will all make sense," Gabe said.

Lee frowned but nodded to Hope to go on.

"The first night I was here in Maxwell I woke up in the middle of the night. I thought I heard someone trying to get into my room. I got out of the bed and went to the door, but by the time I did, the person was long gone. I figured it was just a wrong room or something. There was no reason for me to be particularly alarmed."

"That's possible," Nola said.

"Then last night Gabe and I were going to grab dinner after we left the law office. I wanted to stop by the inn to change clothes. When I went into my room, I noticed that it looked like someone had been tampering with my files. I only had a couple of file folders I left in the room, and there wasn't anything particularly sensitive in them. Nothing was missing, but the papers didn't look quite how I had them. I'm very picky about my files, so that's why I thought something was awry." She looked over at him as if asking if she should recount the close call with the truck. He took over.

"Then when Hope got back into my car for us to hit up Mel's, a truck followed us on our way there. Not just riding too close, but coming within inches of hitting us. I was able to take a quick turn and we lost the guy."

"Why hasn't any of this been reported?" Mike scowled. "You know better, Gabe. You're in private security. You can't just keep this type of stuff to yourself. We're the ones with the duty to protect our citizens and visitors."

"We were going to report all of it today," Hope said. "But I had a meeting first thing with Mr. Nola and I had to attend to that business first. And since I'm from New York, I was a bit hesitant with you thinking that I was imagining things that couldn't possibly happen in Maxwell. Well until this morning."

"We know you didn't imagine the car incident if Gabe was with you," Caleb said.

While Caleb looked like the all American boy next door, Gabe knew he was tough as nails from his military training.

"Which takes me to this morning. I was walking from the inn to the law firm. I didn't think I'd have any reason to need to walk with anyone, so I went by myself. It's not that far, and I assumed I would be perfectly safe. Right before I got into the town square, I was pulled around the corner against the side of the hardware store building. The man had either a knife or gun pushed into my side. He demanded that I tell him where the chip was. I told him I had no idea what he was talking about. Then he claimed that Wakefield stole a chip from Cyber Future."

"And Hope is leaving out the part where the guy almost choked her to death with his forearm. Her neck is badly bruised. You can still see the red marks from the struggle."

The room fell completely silent. All Gabe could hear was the hum of heater.

Lee pounded his fist on the table breaking the intense silence. "We're going to fix this. Chief Winters, I need the full support of the Maxwell Police Department on this."

"You'll have it, Lee. But I must throw something out there, and that is, we don't really have a good understanding of what is happening. We need to conduct an investigation. I would suggest that you let Gabe run his own investigation independent of our department. He'll have more leeway than we will."

"Definitely," Nola said.

Ah, this is just what he was wanting. Access to Nola.

"But first I have to ask you," Caleb said, looking toward Lee. "Is there any truth to this theft claim by Cyber Future's guy? And before you answer, I need to remind you that while I'm your friend, right now I'm acting as police chief. So if you want to talk this over internally for a minute, I will respect that."

No one said a word. Caleb stood up and motioned for Mike to do the same. They walked out of the conference room.

Gabe waited a second and then jumped in, wanting to take control of the situation. "He's right, you know. But irrespective of what you feel comfortable telling the local police, you need to tell me exactly what is going on. If you want me looking out for the best interest of Wakefield Corporation, I need to understand all the angles here. If that means there was a bit of corporate espionage going on, then so be it. But I need to understand the facts to be able to advise you on the security risks to the company and to the players in their individual capacity."

"I'll start." Lee leaned back in the big chair and propped his hands behind his head. "This is the very first I've heard about any of this. I certainly didn't know about any supposed chip stealing. I don't even know what chip they're talking about. So whatever is it, it isn't coming from my office or under my directive. Cyber Future doesn't even have anything we would want!"

"Why don't we start there," Hope said. "Has anyone found anything through this litigation that would give us insight into what chip the Cyber Future guys are talking about?"

"I've heard rumors," Nola said. "I'm sorry, Hope. I didn't tell you earlier, but I wanted to check my sources before I mentioned anything. I didn't want to add misinformation to an already complicated and dangerous situation."

This already started to sound suspect to Gabe. But he was glad that Nola was talking.

"What rumors?" Lee asked.

"That Cyber Future has created a chip that is smarter and better performing than the Wakefield Chip."

"Impossible," Lee snorted.

"Lee, you invented the chip. You're too close to this to be unbiased," Nola said.

The two men exchanged heated looks, and Hope suddenly looked entirely uncomfortable. Not many people would have the guts to talk to the CEO of Wakefield Corporation like that. Nola obviously didn't have any reservations. What did Nola have on Lee?

"Back to the chip." Gabe was trying to get back to the issue at hand.

"Yes," Nola said. "Anyway, if any of that is true, the Cyber Future Chip would be in direct competition with the Wakefield Chip. Cyber Future started as a distribution company but when they acquired that high tech company last year there have been rumors that they have begun developing a highly specialized arm of their business which would be a threat to Wakefield. It's all been very hush hush because Cyber Future is basically running its tech arm like a black box. No information is really coming out of there."

"And why am I the last to hear this?" Lee's voice boomed throughout the conference room.

"I was going to tell you when I had more concrete intel. And after we got done with this trial. I know this lawsuit has been weighing on you. I was trying to protect you. On the stand, you could've said you knew nothing about this if it ever came up."

"How would this be relevant to this lawsuit?" Will asked.

"You never know how tightly a judge is going to rule on relevancy grounds," she said. "It would only take one or two questions to start some trouble."

"Sam needs to get down here now." Lee pulled out his cell.

"Oh, he is. He's flying in tonight instead of tomorrow."

"Carlos," Lee said. "Since you seem to know more than anyone else about all of this. Are you certain that no one at Wakefield has the chip?"

"If they do, they didn't tell me about it."

He said it with ease, but Gabe didn't believe the words out of his mouth. There were far too many neat coincidences.

"Gabe," Lee said. "I want you all over this. Find out exactly what is going on in my company. And stick close to Hope. We can't have our lawyer being attacked on the streets of this town."

"Yes, sir."

"You two get out of here. I'll deal with the police with these two guys, and then I need some time alone to strategize."

"I'll have Sam call you when he gets in tonight. Maybe the two of you can have a late dinner," she said.

"That would be great." Lee stood up and walked over to Hope. He reached out and took her hands.

Gabe felt a flash of jealousy and protectiveness.

"Hope, thank you for everything. I'm so sorry that you've been put into harm's way. Gabe, please watch after her."

"Of course, sir."

They walked out of the conference room and saw Caleb and Mike down the hall. "I think they're ready to talk to you," Gabe said.

"Good. But first I'd like to talk to the two of you. Hope, I plan to use your statement earlier to file a formal report," Caleb said.

She nodded. "Thank you, but I'm not sure what good that will do."

"Just doing things by the book," Mike said.

She slightly raised her eyebrow. Gabe liked the fact that she didn't seem too keen on Mike either. But he couldn't help but have a shred of annoyance toward his good friend Caleb. The way she smiled warmly at him bothered him. He knew it shouldn't. He certainly had no claim on her.

"Hope, I'm sorry your introduction to our town has been so unpleasant." Caleb took a step toward her. "But know that Gabe is really good at his job. If there becomes a time at which you need any protection from our department, we'll be there."

"I don't like the sound of that." She stood with her arms crossed.

"I don't either, ma'am. But we're on the case now. We're going to figure out what is going on in Maxwell."

"Thank you."

Caleb and Mike went back into the conference room. He and Hope made their way outside the building without saying a word. When they got in the car he spoke.

"Hope you're up for some adventure tonight."

"What?" she croaked

* * *

Adventure was about the last thing Hope wanted right now. But here she was standing in the lobby of the Maxwell Inn. Dressed all in black thanks to Gabe's suggestion, waiting for him to pick her up. He'd been very cryptic about what they were going to do. She sure hoped it was legal. Although she figured at the end of the day he was still an FBI agent. Which meant he had to play by the law whether he liked it or not.

She touched her throat, now extremely tender, and flashed back to the morning. She'd never been physically attacked by a person before in her life. Her childhood was filled with emotional abuse but this was a particularly jarring experience. The thought of that man's strong arm pressing the life out of her. Dare she turn to God? Would He listen to her?

It had been a very long time since she'd really even tried to have a serious conversation with God. She'd become totally disconnected from her faith. Not that she even had a very firm foundation in faith to begin with. But a near death experience was starting to make her wonder whether she should rethink that.

One of the main reasons for her disconnect was Barry. He'd been so antagonistic toward her faith. Openly hostile. He'd told her she was a fool for believing in something so irrational. That science alone should dictate how intelligent people think.

It bothered her that she'd been too weak to stand up to him. And look where that all had gotten her. Alone, cheated on, and terribly hurt. She promised herself that she'd start making her own decisions about everything. That included her love life, her career, and most importantly her decisions about faith. So if she wanted to talk to God, there was no one to stop her now.

She wrapped the black scarf around her neck as if that would take away some of the pain. She watched as Gabe's headlights approached.

Walking to the car, she wondered what he had planned for the evening.

"Hey." He smiled at her, instantly putting her at ease.

"You were real tight lipped about this whole thing besides me wearing black."

"I did that just to add a bit of intrigue. Thought you could use a bit of lightening up, given all that's been happening. But we are going to do some recon."

"What kind of recon?"

"Back at Wakefield. We're going to look through Nola's office."

"Are you crazy?" she asked. "Why would we take a risk like that?"

"No, I'm not crazy. And I've been given full security clearance to every part of Wakefield. I spoke to Lee a bit of go and he personally granted the access. I assured him I would be judicious but thorough. He doesn't like the sound of this competitive chip. And he definitely didn't like being in the dark. Especially when his own board member was the one withholding information. There's a bit of distrust brewing between those two."

"Ah, I see now. Lee gave you the green light to snoop on Nola."

"I like that you can put these pieces together. You'd be a good field agent. Ever thought of a career change?"

She laughed. "First I need to find some success in my current career, don't you think?"

"Seems like you're doing pretty good to me. You're second chairing a trial with a hundred million dollar damages claim. If that's not success, then I'm not really sure what is. You've only been at the firm five years."

"That one hundred million dollars number. That's total bogus, you know. They inflated their damages claim. A hundred million dollar verdict would never hold up on appeal given the terms of the contract."

He looked over at her. "It doesn't matter. You wouldn't be here if the partners at the firm didn't think you were up to the task. That speaks a lot for someone who has been at the firm for five years."

"You've been doing your background research on me." She wasn't really surprised. That's exactly what the FBI did. Especially if he ever truly suspected that she would be working in tandem with Nola.

"I'm good at my job too, Hope. You have a solid resume, great law school credentials. Top of your class and all."

"And it's all earned. Nothing I've achieved has come from any favor or any connection. Because I didn't have any. I'm a hard worker. I believe that is half the battle. It's amazing what effort and attention to detail can get you. Particularly as a lawyer."

"On an even more serious topic, how are you feeling from the attack this morning?"

She looked out the car window as he drove. The sun had set and the road wasn't that well lit on the way out to Wakefield. She was grateful that she had Gabe with her. "Do you always carry a weapon?"

"Yes, I do."

"Good."

"You didn't exactly answer my question."

"A wide range of emotions. First, I was in complete shock. I've lived in New York all my life. Born and raised. And I've never had anything remotely like that happen to me there. That's the irony of it all. Come to small town Georgia and get attacked on the street."

"There is more trouble on the horizon in Maxwell. That's for sure." He paused. "Okay, then after the shock how did you feel?"

"Scared. But the fear didn't last as long as I thought it would. Anger came next. Anger at the man who hurt me. Anger at the entire situation. And anger at myself that I didn't have the strength or ability to defend myself."

"Wait, now. None of this is your fault. And it isn't like you had many options. The guy had a weapon on you."

"I've always wanted to take self-defense classes, but would come up with excuses not to sign up for classes. The firm comes first for me. Before everything and anyone—including myself. I thought I didn't have the time or energy to devote to classes. But when I get home, I will definitely be making time. I feel like this entire experience has made me question my priorities a bit. Not that I think they're wrong, but just a bit of reflection. Which I guess is a good thing, if you can say anything good can come out of being accosted. I'm not one to reflect too much. Or think about the past if I can help it."

"Do you go to church? Here in Maxwell most people go to church. All a big part of the southern culture."

How much of her personal life did she want to share with Gabe? He had been a steadying force since she arrived in Maxwell and surprisingly was becoming a friend. But on the other hand, her life was complex. She didn't want to be judged for her choices by this man.

"It's complicated."

He laughed. "That's code for back off, Gabe."

She couldn't help but smile to herself. He had a good sense of humor. "I went to church for a bit. My family wasn't religious at all so I didn't go to church growing up. But in college I met a friend who was involved in campus ministries. So I went with her some while I was in school."

"And then at some point you stopped going?"

"That's the complicated part."

He didn't respond, and she wondered if he was going to let it go.

"If you ever want to talk about it, I'm a good listener. No pressure though." He paused. "I grew up here and church was just a way of life. It was just as much a part of life as going to school, going to work, or going to the grocery store. My dad died when I was pretty young. A massive stroke. Totally unexpected. But my mom and grandma were completely faithful. Church every Sunday without fail. But don't get me wrong. There are church goers in this town who don't exactly lead by example if you know what I mean."

"Yes, I do."

"I'm just telling you all of that so you can understand me a bit better." They pulled into the parking lot at Wakefield. "Here we are. Back to work."

Gabe was an intriguing man. She couldn't help but feel drawn to him. Wanting to know more about him and his life. But for now they had to get to work.

"At least we're not breaking into the building."

He laughed. "No. I wouldn't have made you an accessory to that."

She stepped out of the car and looked up at the main building. Even though it was dark outside, the building was still illuminated. They probably kept lights on twenty-four seven because of security concerns.

"Are there security cameras?"

"Around the main building there are. But there aren't any on that trail we went on or the manufacturing facility. The security threat is deemed to be to the technology in the main building, not the plant workers or the warehouses. All the sensitive technical components are stored in the safes inside. The Wakefield Chip is what has made the company hit the big time, but the other accessories they manufacture also bring in a lot of money. But that's purely a volume product, there's nothing sensitive about them. Hence why they could farm out production to various distributors like Cyber Future."

"You've done a lot of homework," she said.

"It's my job. When I work a case, I don't think any detail is too small. What if that small detail I decide to overlook becomes the eventual key to crack the case? Or worse, what if that piece of information ends up getting someone hurt or killed? I learned that lesson from day one at Quantico."

"If Nola finds out about us snooping in his office, I don't know what he will do."

"I don't plan on having him find out. Let's go inside."

If only she had the same amount of confidence that Gabe did. They walked into the building and the night guard was standing watch.

"She's with me Baxter. Got approval from Lee. Should be in your notes."

"Yes, sir. I personally spoke to Lee earlier. Let me know if you need anything at all. Our mothers have been knitting together a lot lately. I smell trouble. There was talk of us taking part in the play in the spring. You know how early they start practicing each year. Just wanted to warn you."

Gabe laughed loudly. "Thanks for the warning."

"You really do know everyone in this town." She kept up a brisk pace to match his as they walked down the corridor to the elevator.

"Nola's office is on the seventh floor with the rest of the executives."

"And there's no fear that he's in there working?"

"No chance. It's nine o'clock. Why would he be here now? No, he's out trying to hide his tracks somewhere."

They walked to his office and the light was off just as Gabe had predicted. "What are we looking for?"

"Anything that can tie him to the Cyber Future Chip or, frankly, anything illegal. This is a true fishing expedition."

"You're not used to having free reign like this."

"Absolutely not. Having Lee's support is huge. I'll start in the tall filing cabinets, why don't you do the desk, then go to the cabinets in the back and we'll meet in the middle."

"Depending on how much he has this could take a while."

Hope opened the first desk draw. Totally empty besides some hard candy and a few pens. She went to the next draw. Totally empty. The final desk draw had one plain envelope with nothing in it. What kind of person didn't keep anything in their desk? The type of person who was hiding something.

"Gabe, the desk is completely empty."

"Ditto on the file cabinets. He's not stupid. He's been spooked. Probably by what happened to you. I can guarantee he was in this office this afternoon shredding documents."

Her head started to pound. "Document shredding. We're still under a litigation hold. He shouldn't be shredding anything."

Gabe frowned. "Hope, I hate to tell you this, but I don't think abiding by the litigation hold is even on Carlos Nola's radar right now."

"Well what do we do now? This was a useless exercise."

He shook his head. "No, it wasn't. The lack of proof can sometimes be evidence. We know he probably had files in here before. He's a board member. He wouldn't have a completely empty office. That means he was worried about what happened and took some actions. It helps shore up our theory that he's involved in this mess. From top to bottom."

"Our theory?"

"Yeah. I think you were on board with it too."

"Oh, yes, I just wasn't expecting you to give me any credit."

"Why not. You're providing critical insight and information on this case. We're in this together, Hope. Whether you like it or not."

"So are we done here?"

"Inside the main building, but I want to do a swing through the trails and the plant."

She did not want to go back on that trail. But what was she supposed to do? Say she was scared? No way. No. She was a strong, independent woman and she could handle the trail again. She'd have Gabe right there with his gun if anything happened. And nothing was going to.

"You ready?" he asked.

"Yes."

They exited through the back of the building and started walking away from headquarters.

"I've got a flashlight if it gets too dark on the trail. I was hoping there'd be enough moonlight and artificial lighting to avoid that, though."

"You think someone may be around and you don't want them to see us."

"Like I said, I think you missed your FBI career."

She seemed to be earning his respect. Hope was used to having to prove herself time and time again. Working in a big New York City law firm, younger women were often the most underestimated. Being blonde didn't help either. So many people assumed she wasn't smart and had only gotten the job through personal connections. That couldn't be further from the truth. She'd come from nothing and fought for everything she'd ever achieved.

"Gabe, there shouldn't be any plant employees working at this hour. If someone is out there, I don't think they would be friendly."

"Don't worry. I don't think we're going to see anyone. But if we do, let me handle it. Stay right behind me at all times."

"Of course." She had no intention of hanging out on those trails by herself in the middle of the night. "I'm also glad you told me to wear comfortable shoes."

He led the way and they walked in silence away from the headquarters down to the beginning of the trail.

"You good?" he asked.

"Yes. Lead the way. I'll be right behind."

She could hear insects chirping and what she thought was an owl or some other animal. Were there owls in Georgia? She had no idea what she was dealing with. But the thought of random bugs crawling down her arms and falling from the trees really grossed her out. She freely admitted she was a city girl in that respect.

With each step on the narrow trail, she heard the twigs snap under her feet. Even though he was much taller and bigger than her, he somehow knew the trick to being a lot quieter. She sounded like an elephant stomping down the trail.

Being distracted by all the sounds, she didn't focus on getting a firm footing and her ankle twisted. She didn't want to yell out.

So she just stopped for a second to shake it out. He couldn't get too far in front of her.

She flexed and rotated her right foot a few times. Then she put weight on it to make sure she could walk. Yeah, she'd be fine. "Gabe," she whispered.

No answer.

Not wanting to speak any louder, she just kept walking. He couldn't be too much further in front of her. She tried to pick up her pace, but her right ankle started to ache with each additional step.

"Gabe," she whispered again into the darkness.

She took another step and strong arms wrapped around her from behind. One around her neck and the other covering her mouth. Instantly, she started to struggle against him.

"You didn't think you'd get away from me that easily did you, blondie?"

Even though he was behind her, she recognized the voice. It was the man from that morning. He had come back to finish the job. She tried to move but his arm was tight holding her in place. She wouldn't give up though. Not after everything she'd survived in her lifetime.

"There's no point in fighting back. I could snap your neck right now if I wanted to." To make his point, he squeezed her already tender neck even tighter.

Instead of his words instilling fear, they motivated her to fight more. She wanted to live. And she most certainly didn't want to die in these woods tonight at the hands of this evil man.

"Fine," he huffed. "We'll do it your way. But I can't kill you yet. You're coming with me."

She tried to drop lower to the ground making it more difficult for him. He was practically dragging her now through the damp dirt. His one arm so tight across her waist she felt like her ribs were about to crack in two.

Then she heard a noise a bit further away. "Hope!" Gabe's voice rang out.

Before she knew what was happening, her attacker threw her forward with so much force that she landed face down in the wet dirt banging her head against a big rock. Pain shot through her head and her ribs. Then the world went dark.

CHAPTER SIX

Gabe ran as fast as he could. How could he have lost Hope out in the woods? One minute she was right there only a step behind him. The next he had turned around and she had vanished.

His heart pounded and a drop of sweat formed on his brow. He'd promised to protect her. And now she was gone.

"Hope." He yelled. Not a sound in response. Please, Lord, let Hope be all right.

He pulled out his flashlight and started retracing his steps. And that's when he saw her. Hope was crumpled up on the ground.

"Hope, oh please, God, help Hope." He knelt down beside her and immediately checked for a pulse. Thankfully, he felt her pulse. A bit weak but still strong enough.

"Hope, can you hear me?"

He shined the flashlight onto her face and saw the trickle of blood sliding down her cheek. She must have hit her head. Did she trip and fall? Or did someone do this to her? How could he have let this happen?

There was no time for self-recriminations. She needed to get to the emergency room right away. He debated between calling 9-1-1 or taking her himself. He'd had basic medical training and he knew that it might be dangerous to move her without stabilizing her neck. So as much as he wanted to pick her up and carry her to his car, he couldn't risk it.

He pulled out his cell phone and dialed 9-1-1.

"9-1-1, what's your emergency?"

He recognized the older man's voice. "Stan, this is Gabe Marino. I need an ambulance right away sent out to the Wakefield plant. We're back in the trails."

"Are you hurt, Gabe?"

"Not me. It's one of the Wakefield attorneys from out of town. Head injury. Please dispatch them right away."

"They'll be there in no time. I can stay on the line and wait."

"No, I need to tend to her. Just make sure they know we're on the trails, closer to the headquarters side."

"Roger that."

Gabe crouched back down by Hope and said another prayer. He didn't know how bad the head injury was. And since she was unconscious, he had no way of knowing if anything else was hurt.

"Hope, help is on its way. Just stay with me." He grabbed her hand and squeezed. He let out a sigh of relief when he heard the loud sirens.

Within a few minutes, the EMTs were there. All people he knew. He briefed them on the situation. There was no way he was just putting Hope in that ambulance and going home.

He followed the ambulance to the hospital which was a few minutes away. It wasn't a big Atlanta hospital but if the doctors couldn't treat her, they'd send her to Atlanta for sure. He was still praying for a mild concussion and nothing more. But he'd have to wait.

He met Caleb in the hospital waiting room. He walked in frowning.

"What happened out there?" Caleb asked, his blue eyes filled with concern. "Or my first question should be, why were you on the trails in the middle of the night?"

"Keep your voice down, Chief." Gabe figured now wasn't the time to rely on his friendship with Caleb. So he kept things formal. "We were investigating. With Lee's blessing."

Caleb took a step closer to him so that no one could hear their conversation. "This is all tied back up into your Nola investigation, isn't it?"

"This whole Cyber Future Chip thing was totally new to me. But Nola has his hands in it. We checked his office tonight, and it had been wiped clean. Literally no files left in there. He knows something about that Cyber Future Chip for sure. I haven't figured out how that plays into his bigger agenda and other illegal business yet. You and I both know that it has to though."

"I realize you have a job to do for the FBI. But I have a job to do here, too, man. I've got an innocent woman attacked in broad daylight. Now she's in the Maxwell ER. This isn't good for any of us. We need to get a handle on this situation pronto. I don't want to make any more late night ER visits about this. And the trial hasn't even started yet."

"Hope's in danger."

"How did this happen to her anyway. I thought you were sticking close?"

Gabe ran a hand through his hair. "The guilt is eating away at me. She was there with me. One second she was and then the next she wasn't."

"Don't beat yourself up. That won't help anyone. When she regains consciousness, hopefully we'll know a lot more about what happened. But I take it that you don't think she fell?"

"No. It would've had to have been a very hard and awkward fall to knock her out like that. Do you have any local resources you can pull in to put on all the Cyber Future visitors we have in town?"

"You know we're a small police force. Why don't you pull in from the FBI?"

"Do we really want all of that attention? We're so close to busting up Nola's network. An official FBI presence would definitely drive Nola and his people underground."

"What's the alternative?"

"Do all you can with your people, and be strategic about where the resources are placed. Nola's not going anywhere, and he's already on high alert. I think we need to focus on the Cyber Future side for right now. See if we can gain any intel on exactly what they're after."

"If we get in a pinch, I can ask the county sheriff for some folks, too. He owes me from the last time when we lent him resources a missing child case."

Gabe looked over and saw a doctor walking toward them.

"I'm Doctor Miles. You're with the young woman who was brought in?"

"Yes."

"No family here in town?"

"No, she's from New York and in town working on the Wakefield case."

The doctor's eyes lit up with acknowledgment. "Ah, well I can give you the report then. She's sustained a concussion. I'd estimate it to be on the mild side but she still sustained a pretty hard hit to the head. We're in normal care mode for a concussion right now. She'll be kept overnight and re-evaluated in the morning. The other injuries are all minor scrapes and bruises except for some more extensive bruising on the neck."

"She was attacked this morning downtown," Caleb said.

"Seems like this poor girl needs a bodyguard."

"Can we see her?"

"Yes, she's alert. But don't stay too long. She needs to rest."

"Thank you, doctor."

Gabe could barely contain himself as he walked with Caleb down to Hope's hospital room. He stepped inside and took a deep breath. She looked so small and frail lying there in the bed hooked up to the IV. Once again regret ate at him as he couldn't believe he got separated from her in the woods.

He walked over to her bedside and gently took her hand. Her eyes opened quickly.

"It's okay, Hope. You're safe now. It's just Gabe and Chief Winters. Can you tell us what happened to you?"

"The man," she whispered. Her eyes barely opening. "It was the same man from this morning."

"What did he say?"

"He said he couldn't kill me yet because they needed me. I tried to fight back. But he was so strong, there was only so much I could do." She paused and closed her eyes for a second. Then she opened them and looked directly at him. "He heard you coming, Gabe. You saved my life. He was going to kidnap me."

He squeezed her hand. "No, Hope. I should've never let you out of my sight. I don't know what happened. I thought you were right behind me."

"I twisted my ankle. I took a minute to make sure it was okay and that's when you got ahead of me. I didn't call out to you because I didn't want anyone to hear."

"You were very smart and very brave. We're going to catch this guy."

"Let me echo that, Hope. I'm so sorry again that all of this has happened to you. Gabe isn't going to take his eyes off of you again, are you, Gabe?"

"No, sir. You're stuck with me, Hope. Until this gets sorted out."

"My head hurts," she said weakly.

"You need to rest. You have a concussion."

"Don't leave."

"I'm not going anywhere, Hope. You can count on that." And he meant it.

***

Hope's head ached and her neck burned. But she felt cold all over. Then it hit her. As the sunlight burst through the window, she remembered what an awful day yesterday was. She definitely wasn't in her bed in New York. Not even in her bed at the inn. No, she was in the hospital.

Straining her neck she tried to lift up a little. That's when she saw him. Gabe was hunched over in the chair. His hair slightly tussled. He'd stayed the night right by her side. Just like he said he would. She felt a bit guilty for him having to sleep in the chair, but given what she'd been through she also couldn't stand the thought of being alone.

That man had come after her twice now. With the clear intent to hurt her. But not only to hurt her. He'd kill her when she was no longer of use to him. A chill shot through her just thinking about it, and her head throbbed with pain. She'd hit the ground hard.

Gabe groaned and opened his eyes. For a moment, she saw the confusion on his face as he narrowed his eyes.

"How are you feeling?" he asked.

"I've been better."

"You had a tough fall. I have to apologize again."

"No you don't. You're the reason I'm here in the hospital bed right now and not already dead."

"If I wouldn't have let you walk behind me, you wouldn't be in either scenario." He stood up from the chair and walked over to the bed.

"The blame game won't help either of us. We need to figure out what is going on before someone really gets hurt. I don't think I'm the only one in danger here."

"I'm going to start calling you Agent Finch."

She smiled.

"I knew I could get you to smile."

"What is Nola going to do when he finds out we were snooping around on the trails last night?"

"I've got a cover story. Lee is setting it up. Saying that he wanted me to check out the security situation at night. And you were just with me because I didn't want to let you be alone after what happened."

"Regardless, he'll be skeptical. The fact that he cleaned out his office lets us know he's worried about something."

He leaned in closer to her. "I see two issues at play here. The first is Nola's crime ring. The second is the theft of the Cyber Future Chip and all that flows from it."

"And you think the two have to be connected."

"I think you do, too. The way I see it, we have a couple of issues of commonality. Nola being the obvious. The fact that they're focused on you is giving me some pause. Maybe they think you're involved with Nola. Since I thought it was a possibility, they might think the same thing. You could be helping with the legal work to cover up his illegal activity."

"That means they have found out somehow that I work with Nola and not just generally on this case. How would they have found that out?"

"People talk in this town. That much I can say for sure. Could have even been an innocent comment about what you were working on. But once that information got into Cyber Future's hands they went with it."

"And you're comfortable with the notion that the actual company hired that man to come after me?"

"It's the only scenario that really makes sense. An individual wouldn't have any incentive to do so. Why would a random man care about who has the chip? No, it has to be Cyber Future. Which gets us back to what Nola did and whether he has the chip."

"And what he plans to do with it," she said quietly.

"You don't need to worry about all of that right now. You need to rest and get your strength back." He grabbed her hand and squeezed. "I've asked Caleb to station an officer outside your door. I need to leave for just a little bit to try to track some things down and to give my boss a full debrief."

"Are you sure I'll be safe?"

"Yes. That officer won't let anyone in here that isn't authorized. He has strict orders."

"All right," she said reluctantly.

He smiled at her. "Get some rest. I'll be back soon."

She nodded and realized how much her head still ached. Closing her eyes, she wondered how it had come to this. Now wasn't the time to overanalyze, though. Gabe was right. She needed to rest.

A loud buzzing sound awakened her from a deep sleep. What in the world? Then she realized it was the fire alarm. It had to be.

She sat up in the bed and realized she had to move. Where was everyone?

Thankfully, just when she was starting to feel abandoned, a nurse dressed in green scrubs came into the room. He would help her get out safely. But when she looked up into his eyes, her stomach dropped. Instant recognition. This was her attacker.

"Screaming won't do you any good." He stepped toward her with a needle in his hand. What was he going to inject her with?

"No," she yelled.

"Everyone is evacuating. The stupid cop is gone. He thought I was coming in here to get you, so he went to help others get out. It's just you and me now, blondie. After last night do you really want to try and fight me? Just calm down and we can get out of here nice and easy."

"Why are you doing this? I already told you I don't know anything."

"I don't believe you. And even if I did, it doesn't matter what I think. I'm just following orders. I don't plan to get killed. So I need to bring you in. It's as simple as that. You have proven to be a bit more fight than I expected, especially for a woman your size.

But how difficult you want to make it on yourself is purely up to you. The end result will be the same."

She looked at the man. He could've just been your average guy walking down the street. He was tall with dark hair and brown eyes. Clean cut and pretty normal looking. But she knew better. He was a killer for hire. Or at the very least a hired gun of some sorts. His comments confirmed that.

Making a split second decision, she knew what she needed to do.

"But I will tell you that it will be much easier for you if you just hold still. I'm not trying to cause you more trouble than I have to." He stepped closer to the bed and leaned down with the needle.

Once he stuck her with that needle, she would be dead. Maybe not right that minute, but she couldn't let him take her out of that hospital. *Please, Lord, give me strength.* Would He hear her prayer?

One more step and the man's hands were almost touching her. That's when she made her move. With her left arm she went for his right hand holding the needle, and landed a direct blow. She heard the needle hit the floor.

His dark eyes widened in shock, but he quickly recovered. Grabbing her off the bed. She started kicking and screaming. Trying her best to try to yell over the blaring fire alarm. Would anyone hear her?

Regardless, she refused to give up. She was thrashing and kicking with all of her might throwing him a little off balance. Yes, he was strong, but she was unwieldy.

He tightened his grip on her and she yelped. But that only drove her to fight more. She dug her fingernails into his back. Desperate for any chance to get away.

"Put her down," a loud voice boomed. "I will shoot."

Gabe, she realized. Thank you, God.

The man dropped her down unceremoniously onto the bed and turned around.

"Hands in the air where I can see them."

The man raised his hands in the air. "I don't think you're really going to use that."

"Don't test me. On your knees. Hands behind your head."

Hope watched as Gabe pulled out handcuffs from his jacket pocket and placed them on the man.

"Hope, are you all right?" he asked.

"Yes. I'm okay."

The fire alarm blaring stopped. They must have figured out it was a false alarm. No doubt set off by her attacker.

Gabe pulled out his cell, and she heard him talking to Caleb. Within a few minutes, her attacker was escorted out by the Maxwell police. Caleb and Gabe were talking in hushed tones right outside her hospital door. A nurse was busy checking her out. Her head was pounding, but she insisted she was fine. She strained to try to listen to Gabe and Caleb's conversation. She hated being kept in the dark. Especially when she was the exact topic of the conversation.

"Hey, guys. Want to fill me in?" she asked loudly.

Gabe frowned and walked into her room with Caleb right behind. It was Caleb who spoke first.

"I am so sorry, Hope." His light blue eyes seemed kind as he talked in a quiet voice. "My officer should have never left the door. Regardless of the circumstance. I will speak to him and make sure he understands the gravity of what could've happened here today."

"He was tricked. I'm sure he thought that the attacker was a nurse who was going to get me out. He had no way of knowing it wasn't a real fire. He was just trying to help."

"That's no excuse," Gabe said. "If I wouldn't have come back when I did, you'd be gone by now and we'd have no way of finding you."

"Let's not even think about that."

"Unfortunately, we have to, Hope." Gabe sat down on the edge of her bed.

"We're going to fully interrogate this guy. But in my experience he's either going to lawyer up or clam up. Or both. He'll have the resources for a good lawyer that's for sure. We'll do our best though to get any information from him that could help."

"The bottom line is that just because he's in custody doesn't mean you're safe." Gabe reached over and touched her forearm. "Cyber Future thinks you're the key here to whatever it is they need."

Hope looked up at the hospital door and saw Sam Upton. Uh oh, this wasn't going to end well.

"Hope," he said. He rushed toward her but was stopped by Caleb. "Sir?"

"It's okay, it's Sam Upton. The partner on the Wakefield litigation. My boss."

"I'm Chief of Police Caleb Winters and this is a private security consultant Gabe Marino." Sam shook hands with both of them. He looked at Caleb, then Gabe, and then finally back to her. "Hope, what in the world is going on?"

"It's a long story, Sam."

"Are you all right?"

Before she could answer, Gabe stood up. "Sam, your case has gotten a lot more complicated, even more so in the past few hours."

"How so? And how does Hope play into this?"

"The man who attacked Hope claims that Wakefield stole a computer chip from them. A highly proprietary and cutting edge innovation."

"Yes, I heard about all of that already. What I don't understand is why he keeps coming after Hope. That man made another attempt at her life just now in this hospital? How did that happen Chief Winters?"

"He used the fire alarm as a diversion tactic, and my man guarding the door took the bait."

Sam started pacing back and forth around the hospital room. "I have been practicing law for thirty years, and I have never had anything like this ever happen. The life of one of my employees is in danger. I need to do something about that. No." He paused. "I *have* to do something about that."

A chill shot down her arm. She'd never seen Sam even close to losing his cool. He was always the one who was the sturdy force even during the most trying cases. But right now the stress and concern filled the room. Sam clenched his fists and continued to pace.

Caleb took a step toward Sam. "Mr. Upton, I know you are rightfully concerned about Hope's safety. But you need to let us do our jobs on that front."

"Like you've been doing a good job at that? No. Hope, don't you want to go back to New York?"

She shook her head. "Trial starts Monday. I'm not going anywhere."

Sam walked over to her bedside. "Hope, if something happens to you, I'll never forgive myself. There's not a single case that is more important than your life."

"We'll be much more prepared for the threat now, sir," Gabe said. "If Hope wants to stay, we will protect her. I will protect her."

Sam shook his head. "I have an awful feeling about this. Hope, given all that's happened have you even had a chance to work with Nola?"

"Yes, we did. I'm not too worried about his testimony." At least not specific to the breach of contract. If opposing counsel was allowed to inquire about the chip, that would be a different story.

"I'm going to meet with Lee again. I saw him last night, but I want to make sure everything is taken care of. When are you they releasing you?"

"Hopefully today."

"Okay. I'll be at either Wakefield or the Trent firm if you need me." Then he turned to Gabe and Caleb, his face red. "You two better keep to your word about keeping her safe. A lawsuit brought by my firm would only be the beginning of your problems."

The room fell silent after Sam left. She couldn't stand it any longer and wanted to break it. "So what now?" she asked. "I'm ready to get out of here."

"Are you sure you're ready for that?" Gabe asked. "You've been through a lot."

"Yes. I can do more to help if I'm out of this hospital."

"Hope, you should be focusing on your job and let us focus on ours," Caleb said.

"No. My job is tied up in your job. And I was brought into this from day one by the FBI. Don't think I've forgotten about that."

"That was before you were a target," Gabe said.

"What? You also want me to step back and run away? The guy is in custody."

"There are a million more hit men that Cyber Future could hire."

Hit men. The enormity of the situation hit her. But she couldn't back down. "If that's true, then you know as well as I do that I'm not safe. They'll track me down wherever I am. This is the safest place for me. Returning to New York right now isn't even an option in my mind."

"I can see this is a complex and messy situation. I'm headed back to the station to interrogate our guy. I'll be in touch." Caleb walked out leaving her alone with Gabe.

"You know I'm right," she said.

"Yeah, but it doesn't mean I have to like it. That was far too much of a close call earlier."

She let out a breath. "I know, but thankfully you showed up."

"By the grace of God. I can't even fathom the alternative."

A doctor walked into the room. "Ms. Finch, are you ready for your exit exam?"

She nodded and felt a shred of relief that she was getting out of there.

***

Gabe said a prayer feeling like the weight of the world was on his shoulders. He'd almost lost Hope again today. He didn't want to admit it, but he thought he might have started to develop some feelings for her. It was probably just a function of his protective instincts. But it bothered him the same.

His mission was clear, though. He had to not only protect her, but find answers, or there would be no way to keep her safe.

As they sat at Mel's regrouping and getting some solid food into her, his mind went through a million different scenarios.

"I'm glad you're eating." He watched as she took a huge bite out of her barbeque sandwich.

"I'm actually ravenous." She picked up a fry slathered in ketchup.

"You need your strength, so eat up."

At least a bit of color was coming back to her cheeks. He hated seeing the bandage that was still above her right eye. She'd hit the ground hard. It could've been much worse. That's what he had to keep reminding himself.

She sighed and put down her sandwich. "You know when that guy came into my room today at first I didn't know it was him. Then I looked into those eyes, and I really thought it was all over. I prayed for a burst of strength."

"And what happened?"

"I was able to knock the needle out of his hand. I just knew that if he drugged me and took me out of the hospital it was only a matter of time before they killed me." She looked down and then back up at him, her brown eyes glistening with tears.

"But you didn't die." He reached over the table and grabbed her hand. "You're here and you're here for a reason. We may not understand exactly how God works, Hope. But I'm sure that He was watching over you today."

"I feel that way too. I don't have a rational explanation for it, but I just sense His presence."

He reluctantly let go of her hand. "We need to talk about how we move forward."

"Do you think the man who attacked me is going to talk to the police?"

"I could lie to you and say yes to try to make you feel better, but I'd rather just tell you the truth. I think the chances are slim to none."

"I was afraid of that."

"Don't let that thought spoil your appetite."

"Think about it, though. Most normal corporations may engage in shady or even illegal business practices—tax evasion, corporate loopholes, even white collar crime. But ordering hits on people is on a different level. That means that Cyber Future may be operating in tandem with a criminal enterprise."

"You're thinking ties to organized crime?" he asked.

"Aren't you?"

He took a bite of his jumbo barbeque sandwich and gave it some thought. If Hope was right, then the situation could be even more dangerous than he'd envisioned. Corporate espionage gone too far is one thing. But if this was all tied up to the mob, that was something else. "It's a viable theory."

"This could be a battle between two organized crime factions," she said.

"Nola has managed to get Wakefield involved probably unbeknownst to anyone else on the Board of Directors. And we really have no concept about what is happening over at Cyber Future."

"Except that they're willing to kill over that chip."

"And they think you're involved with Nola."

Silence fell between them as he looked into her eyes. It really hit him that he not only felt the need to protect her but something more. An ever growing feeling. One that wouldn't subside.

She broke the silence. "Where does that leave me?"

"For one, I'm not leaving you alone. I'll get an adjoining room at the inn and make sure you're safe. I'll be your constant shadow. I will not fail you again."

"Gabe, you didn't fail me. So don't even say that. I will tell you that these two near misses have led me to re-examine some things."

"What type of things?"

"My relationship with God."

"The complicated one." He smiled.

"You remembered that comment? It's still complicated. But the fact that I'm still alive means something. At least to me."

"Of course it means something."

"Don't think I didn't notice that you kept Sam in the dark about your FBI status."

"It's better if the circle is as small as possible. It's the only way to really keep my cover intact. Now that's more important than ever. Especially if we're caught up in something bigger than I originally anticipated. Nola pushing some illegal businesses into Maxwell is troubling. But my boss may want to bring in additional resources if he buys into this dueling crime ring theory."

"This trial is starting Monday whether we like it or not."

"You need some rest. Doctor's orders for that concussion. Let's head back to the inn."

"I guess I can't argue with that."

They walked out of Mel's into the cool January evening. He stuck close to Hope as they walked the short distance toward his car.

A sound of screeching tires tore through the night, and he prayed he wouldn't be too late as he dove forward.

CHAPTER SEVEN

ope heard the loud squealing noise, but before she could register what was happening Gabe pushed her down. She hit the ground hard with the breath knocked out of her.

She opened her eyes just in time to see the car speed off down the street. Her heart pounded and she realized that Gabe was holding onto her.

"Are you okay?" he asked, his voice ragged.

She tried desperately to steady her breathing. The reality of the situation hit her. Someone had tried to run them over. Or more likely, run her over. "You saved my life."

"Barely. That was a close call. He literally came out of nowhere. By the time I heard the tires, it was almost too late."

She did not want to cry but the enormity of what she faced began to sink in, and she wiped a stray tear from her cheek.

"Did you hit your head?"

"No, most of the impact was on my arm and shoulder."

"I'm sorry I hit you so hard."

"No, like I said, you saved my life."

"Do you want to go back to the hospital and get checked out?"

"No." She shook her head. "I definitely don't want to do that. I just want to rest in my own hotel room and have a bit of alone time."

"I totally understand. I'll get you back to the inn, and then I'll report this to Caleb."

"So they've already started again. They didn't waste any time."

"Come on, let's go to the car, and we can talk in there."

She nodded and walked slowly to the car. Her life had turned into a nightmare since she stepped foot into Maxwell. Which was a shame because the town itself was growing on her.

She was thankful when Gabe turned the heat on in the car. She felt a chill wash over her body. It was to be expected, given what she'd been though. Her head started to pound.

"They really think you know something. If they are so desperate that they are now willing to injure or kill you without getting information from you first that says a lot."

She grimaced. "Thanks."

"No. I didn't mean it like that. The last thing I want to do is upset you. But you're really smart, Hope. You would've figured that out for yourself anyway. What I need you to do is to start racking your brain. Maybe you will think of something that can tie you to whatever they want beyond just you working with Nola. Something you saw or read, something you had access to that they think you looked at. Anything. Even if it seems trivial, you need to let me know. We might be making the wrong assumptions about this chip and what it contains."

She sighed. "I really want to know, too. I keep thinking but nothing stands out. I'll keep going over it in my mind and let you know if I come up with any ideas."

She looked over at him as he kept his eyes on the road. She could tell he had a tight grip on the wheel. No doubt still on high alert. And thankfully he'd had the presence of mind to knock her out of the way earlier. Saving them both in the process.

When would this awful nightmare end?

After only a few minutes, they arrived at the inn.

"I'm going to get a room next to yours. Let me check out your room first though."

As they got out of the car, she noted that he was on edge. Ready and watching their surroundings. He put his hand on her back and guided her into the lobby. Constantly surveying the area and her at the same time.

It was in that moment that something hit her. She was starting to care for this man. Was it just her seeing him as her strong protector? Or was there something deeper? If something did develop, he would end up hurting her just like Barry, wouldn't he?

She shook off those thoughts and tried to focus on her immediate problem. Not getting killed. Never in a million years would she have imagined that she could've ever been in danger like this over a case she worked on. She wasn't a prosecutor. It wasn't like she put criminals away for a living. She practiced boring business litigation. Or at least it had been boring until now. Until hired assassins tried to kill her.

By the time she sat down on her hotel room bed, she had worked herself up. She was no longer tired, but angry. There was a knock at the door and she walked over and looked out the peep hole.

"It's Gabe."

Her eyes confirmed what she heard and she opened the door letting him in.

"I'm right next door. I don't want you to answer the door for anyone but me. You got that?"

"Definitely. I was so worn out but now I think it's too early to go to sleep."

"Wow. You've got one of the bigger rooms here. A separate living room."

"Yeah, for working if I need to."

"You want some company?"

"Sure, maybe we can have them send up some hot tea. Don't you need to talk to Caleb?"

"Yeah, and in fact, he may want to come over here to get your statement anyway."

"Why don't you contact Caleb, and I'll call down for the tea."

He nodded and pulled out his cell phone. Maybe it would be a good thing for Caleb to come over to the inn. They needed a plan.

In less than half an hour, the three of them were seated at her table with tea in front of them and frowns all around.

"Hope, walk me through what happened at Mel's."

"First let me apologize. I'm sorry to have pulled you away from your family tonight."

"It's just me and my dog so don't you worry about that. I fed him dinner so he was ready for a good ole' nap curled up in front of the TV. And Gabe, I was able to get Zeke brought over to my house so you can stay here with Hope."

"Thanks," Gabe said. "Zeke loves hanging at your place. Caleb is my pet sitter when I have to travel for work."

"Ok, Hope. Let's hear it," Caleb said.

Hope looked at Caleb. She couldn't believe that the chief of police in Maxwell was single. There had to be a backstory involved. For now though she was going to focus on her issues. "We had just finished dinner. I know I wasn't particularly on guard or anything. I had no idea that something could happen again so fast."

"Take me through it slowly."

"We walked out of the door of the restaurant. We were about halfway to Gabe's car, which was parked toward the edge of the lot when I heard the very loud squeal of tires. The next thing I know, Gabe was on top on me and I was on the ground. He pushed me out of the way and saved my life."

"I reacted. Pure and simple," Gabe said.

"He's trying to downplay it, but if he wouldn't have reacted we'd both probably be dead or gravely injured."

Caleb nodded. "Which direction did the car come from?"

"When we were walking to the car, we walked through the parking lot. I was on the left and Gabe was on the right. Gabe was closer to the street. The car came from his side, and he pushed me out of the way forward and to the left."

"Did you see the car?"

"Yes. Only after I was on the ground, though. I looked up and saw it speeding off down the road going left down the street. It was a dark sedan. But beyond that, I couldn't give a better description."

"I spoke to Lee on the way over here. He's very concerned about you. As is your boss."

"We've been over this before. If I go back to New York, I'll be a sitting duck. I'm safer here with Gabe." Had she just said that? It was the truth whether she wanted it to be or not.

"I agree. But they're both very nervous about the start of the trial on Monday. I assured them we would have extra security at the courthouse. I've contacted the county sheriff for additional personnel. For the sake of all involved."

"Anything else on Nola?" Gabe asked.

"No. He's really good at covering up his tracks. I don't know who all he has working for him, but they're running a professional operation. Nola is important, but right now I want to neutralize this Cyber Future threat. We can handle Nola. At least he's not running around attacking people."

Gabe frowned. "I don't like hearing that, but you're right. The most imminent threat right now is from Cyber Future."

"We have to figure out what is on that chip. Or what that chip can do. It has to be important." Hope poured more tea and took a sip. Figuring out that chip was the key to her safety.

"All right. Well, it's getting late," Caleb said. "Hope, I'm sure you're exhausted. And again I'm sorry that your time in our town has been so awful. I promise you it's not normally like this here. We're a quiet and peaceful place. Well, it was until Nola's business sprung up. But even that wasn't to the extent of what's happening now."

"I'm going to need to go into the law firm tomorrow and get some work done," she said.

"That's fine. Just make sure Gabe is with you wherever you go. I know it's very constraining to have a shadow, but it's necessary right now."

"No, I get it."

Caleb stood up and patted her shoulder before he walked out of the room.

"I want to echo what Gabe said. I had no idea things were going to escalate the way they have. This Cyber Future angle has really thrown me."

"Believe me. I'm aware of how serious this is. But on the other hand, I still have a trial. A trial that I earned second chair in, and I don't want to mess up this opportunity. These chances don't come around every day for a lawyer working in a large New York firm."

"I'd think you would get to go to court a lot."

She shook her head. "Not in my line of work. Most of our cases settle or get resolved well before trial. Jury trials are rare. So when the opportunity presents itself you really have to jump on it. And as a fifth year lawyer, having a seat at counsel's table is pretty much an impossibility. That's why this means so much to me. The experience will be an invaluable piece to add to my resume."

"How did you manage to get second chair?"

"The other partner who had worked on the case had an international arbitration that Sam wanted him to attend. Since I'm the associate who worked the case and was familiar with the client, they elevated me to second chair. Sometimes doing the grunt work and being the contact for all the client's questions pays off."

"I get the impression that you work a lot."

She laughed. "Work is my life."

He looked at her, his eyes filled with interest. "Does that life-style make you happy?"

"Of course," she answered without thinking. "My lifestyle not only makes me happy, it's necessary."

"What do you mean?"

"My family didn't have much when I was growing up, so I promised myself that I would be totally independent and never worry about money. If that means working eighty hours a week at the firm, then so be it."

"That's a lot of pressure to put on yourself."

"Actually it's better than you might think. It would be more pressure to worry about finances. I will live in New York and make partner within a few years. I have it all planned out."

"It's good you have a plan. And I'm glad you like being a lawyer. I feel the same way about my work. But there's a piece of me that sometimes whispers that I want something more. Or at least someone to share life with."

Whoa. She wasn't expecting this turn in the conversation. For some reason though, she felt comfortable talking to him about it. "My track record with men hasn't been a sterling one. It's just better for me to focus on my career and putting money in savings and that sort of thing."

"We all have our past issues."

"I trusted someone and he broke my heart. Another lawyer in New York."

He reached over and touched her hand. "He must have been an idiot."

"An unfaithful idiot."

"Hope, I'm so sorry. No one deserves to be cheated on."

"So after that debacle, I've taken a break from dating. It's just easier to not engage at all. Focus on work and then maybe one day when I'm ready I'll figure out how to get back out there."

"It's natural to be hurt. And cautious. But not every man is like your ex-boyfriend. You deserve someone who is going to treat you with the respect you deserve."

Enough about her. "What about you?"

"I could take your line and say it's complicated. But that wouldn't be fair given you shared your experiences with me." He leaned forward in his chair. "Unlike a lot of people I have no problem being alone. I have to be a people person in some aspects of my job, but in my personal life I'm fine with a very small circle of family and friends. And according to some, I have been known for being a bit picky."

She smiled. "Really? I can see that."

"Don't get me wrong. I don't expect perfection. No one's perfect. Most certainly not me. But I also believe there's someone out there who has everything I want. Some people have certain qualities and not others. I want it all."

"And what would those qualities be?"

"Someone who is smart and passionate about what she cares about. Someone who understands how important my work is. But she also needs to be kind and caring, funny, and love animals."

"Yes, your dog, Zeke."

He looked down and back up. "I just lost my golden retriever a few months ago. He was old and battling cancer. I thought I needed time to grieve. But the house just seemed too empty without him. So I went to animal control and adopted a Labrador. No one can replace my golden, but a man should have a dog. And a family should have a dog. So that's how I ended up with Zeke."

This man was breaking her heart and filling it up at the same time. It wasn't every day that she met someone like Gabe Marino. "You're an interesting man, Gabe."

He grinned. "I hope that you mean interesting in a good way."

"I do." She paused. "I love dogs and cats. But I haven't had a pet since law school. My roommate had a cat that I adored. I've never had one of my own. My family didn't have extra money for pets. My parents could barely afford to feed me."

He narrowed his eyes at her. "You're a tough lady."

"I've had to be."

"I'm going to keep you safe, Hope." He grabbed her hand again and squeezed. "I'd better let you get some rest. We'll go to the firm in the morning whenever you're ready."

"Thanks. And thanks for the talk. It was nice to think about something other than being targeted by a hit man."

"Of course. I'm right next door if you need anything. And don't open that door."

"Goodnight, Gabe."

He stood up and walked out of her room. She couldn't help the feeling that she didn't want him to go. She felt safe with this man. Protected. Something she had truly never felt. Barry had been nice at first. A total romantic—or at least she thought. Huge bouquets of flowers sent to her office, romantic dinners at fancy New York restaurants. Looking back now, though, she realized that those were all empty gestures. He didn't truly love her.

Even worse, he'd used her and made her feel bad about herself. Barry and Gabe couldn't have been more different. Yes, they were both handsome men, but that was where the similarity stopped. Barry acted like he was smarter than everyone, but he wasn't that intelligent. Barry might have tried to romance her, but he was not a gentleman. And of course the cruelest part of all was his infidelity. Something that he didn't even think was a big deal. His words rang over and over in her mind. *Why are you so upset, Hope? She didn't mean anything.* Yeah right.

She shook her head, remembering how those words had hit her like a blow to the gut. It was in that moment that she knew he would keep cheating on her because he saw nothing wrong with it. He was completely devoid of any moral compass. That was one of the things that drew her to Gabe. He was the type of man who wanted to do the right thing. Someone with integrity. With strong faith.

But she needed to stop having these delusional thoughts about Gabe. She'd heard him. He wanted a woman who had it all put together and would sit back and accept his FBI lifestyle. She was still trying to figure out her life. A life that was firmly engrained at the law firm and living in New York City. They would never work. Just because they got along now, didn't man their lives were compatible with each other. Not to mention how they were raised so differently. Her a poor girl in the big city. Gabe in small town Georgia.

He would never live in New York, and she surely didn't want to move. She'd meant what she had explained to him about her lifestyle. A little crush wasn't going to change that.

***

When Gabe heard the scream, he awoke with a start. Going into autopilot, he jumped out of bed and ran next door to Hope's room. Her door was shut, so he banged on it. Not getting an immediate answer, he took a few steps back, ready to ram it open with his shoulder.

Then the door opened revealing Hope standing there wrapped tightly in a robe with tears streaming down her face.

"What happened?" He walked into her room looking for the assailant.

"It was just an awful nightmare."

A flood of relief soared through him. "I heard you scream and feared the worst."

"I'm sorry to have woken you."

"No, I'm fine. Do you want to talk about the nightmare?"

She sat down in one of the chairs and looked up at him. He could see the fear in her eyes and it killed him.

"It was so real. Like I was reliving the attacks. I'm sorry. I know it probably seems a bit melodramatic to be in tears. But it was so emotional. You probably think I'm crazy."

He walked over and knelt down beside her. "I don't think you're crazy. You've been through more trauma in one day than most people do in a lifetime. I'd think there was something wrong with you if you didn't have some sort of visceral reaction."

"You've been so kind to me."

"You deserve that and more. If I could've prevented any of this I would have."

"You're a good man, Gabe Marino."

She had him up on a pedestal. He had his flaws, more than a few. "Just trying my best. That's all anyone can ask of us. You should try to go back to sleep. It's just two a.m."

"Maybe the worst is over." Her voice shook as she spoke.

"I'm right next door. Don't hesitate to call if you need me. I'll be right over."

Gabe didn't sleep much the rest of the night. On edge. Worried about her. He prayed for strength and guidance. He knew Caleb had been right. The priority had to be shifted to the Cyber Future Chip investigation. Nola would have to be secondary. Because the Cyber Future guys had their sights on Hope.

He ran through the possible connections that Cyber Future could have with organized crime. They were a California based company and the most powerful organized crime groups in that area had ties to the Asian crime rings. Was it possible that the Asian and Italian mafia were having a fight over a very valuable computer chip? Nola might be in over his head. Yeah Nola was bad news and definitely had ties to organized crime, but the powerful groups operating in California were on a different level. It would definitely add up that they would be willing to put a hit out on Hope if they thought she was the key to the chip.

Those thoughts were still in the forefront of his mind as he guided Hope into the law office the next morning.

"Nola is coming in to talk about his examination," Hope said. She hadn't slept well either. The dark circles under her eyes and lack of color in her cheeks told him that.

"Since it's Friday, I guess that makes sense. Greg's not been around much lately."

"He's just our local counsel. I don't know how familiar you are with that practice, but we needed a local firm to be able to work with to try the case. But it's pretty common for local counsel to take a more limited role. He's there if we need him. And he and Lee are obviously friends."

He closed the door to Hope's office. "Before Nola gets here, I wanted to run some ideas by you."

"All right." She sat down at the desk across from him. Today she wore a simple but classy black pantsuit and blue blouse.

"I've been thinking a lot about the battling organized crime groups theory. And given Cyber Future's home office, I think it's most likely that there's a connection to the Asian organized crime groups. Now that is not my area of specialty. I'm much more familiar with the traditional mafia groups and to a lesser extent the Russian groups. But here, I think it makes the most sense."

"And you think one of those groups is working with Cyber Future?"

"Yes. Even if it's not an entire group, maybe someone from the group or an offshoot is. Whoever it is, whether it's supported by a traditional style organization or a rogue operation, it's the scenario that makes the most sense. Random criminals aren't this persistent. They certainly don't put out hits and keep coming back in the face of danger and the real possibility of being caught."

"That all sounds like a solid working theory. But we're still at a loss for figuring out how I come into play."

"When was the last time you saw Nola before you came to Maxwell?"

"It was about a week before. He was in New York on other business. I took him to dinner and we had meetings at the firm."

He nodded. "I need you to think back to both the meetings and the dinner. Did you notice anything suspicious? Anyone watching you?"

"You have to remember, I wasn't in high alert mode then. I was just doing my job, focusing on making the client happy. I don't remember anything out of the ordinary."

"When you met with him, did he give you anything?"

"What do you mean? Like what?"

"Anything at all."

She sat in silence with a frown pulling at her lips.

"Think, Hope. Take all the time you need." He could hear the clock on the wall ticking as Hope racked her brain.

Then her eyes widened. "Yes. He did."

"What? What did he give you?"

"When we were at dinner, right before we were done, he gave me a small USB drive. He said it contained copies of the documents he'd brought to our office in hard copy that day. I didn't think anything of it."

"What did you do with the drive?"

"I sent it to our file room at the firm. It should be filed with the case file. Oh no." She paused. "We had all the case files shipped down here."

"Where are those?"

"They're being stored at the client's. There wasn't enough room here for all of them, so we only have the witness preparation files and trial exhibits here on site. All the backup and the rest of the case files are at Wakefield."

"That has to be it, Hope." His pulse raced. This was just the break he needed. "We need to get over to Wakefield and search for that drive. Does anyone know what you did with the drive?"

"My secretary sent it to the file which is our usual procedure. I give it to her and she makes sure it is filed. No one else would've known about it."

"And Nola. Has he asked you about it?"

"Not yet."

"Someone had eyes on you at that dinner in the restaurant. That's why you're being targeted. The chip information has to be on that drive."

A loud knock made Hope jump. "Sorry, I'm a little skittish."

The door opened and Nola walked in. "Are you ready for me?"

"Yes, I am."

"Good morning, Gabe. Any security updates?" Nola asked.

"My biggest concern right now is keeping Hope safe. She's obviously been targeted by Cyber Future because they think she has something to do with this chip. Have you given it any more thought? Any ideas on how they get her roped into this?"

Nola didn't flinch. "No. It's a total mystery to me. And it angers me that they continue to come after her. Why don't we hire additional private security for the balance of the trial? I'm sure Wakefield will more than cover the cost."

"We're considering all options at this point."

"Good. Now I guess we have some other work to attend to, Hope?"

"Yes," she said. Her legal pad was in front of her and her laptop sat opened. She was the ever competent attorney ready to prepare her witness.

"There's something I've decided that I should tell you before you put me on the stand."

Gabe stood up, realizing it was his time to exit.

"What?" she asked leaning forward.

He closed the door. What he wouldn't give to be a fly on the wall.

CHAPTER EIGHT

"**C**yber Future is right about the breach of contract. That was my doing."

"What did you say?" Hope asked. She had to have heard Nola wrong.

"I figure with everything else going on, now is the time to come clean about the contract."

"What did you do, Carlos?" she asked, purposely using his first name. She could feel the trial crumbling right in front of her. All of the work, the hours, and the stress, and now this.

Nola crossed his arms in front of him. "Remember I told you how I thought getting involved with Cyber Future was an awful idea. I tried to convince Lee that they were bad news. As a side note, I was right about all of it. Just look at what is happening now. Lee should've listened to me."

"Let's get back to what you did with the contract." She wanted to hear this.

"I got tired of the Cyber Future nonsense. So their allegations are factually accurate. We stopped payment and diverted our supply of the Wakefield Chip to one of their competitors."

She was at a loss. "But the documents, I've seen them all. We have records of paying them the full amount owed."

"Those were forged."

She put her head in her hands. How had she gotten involved in this? A board member of her client was admitting to forging documents? "Does Lee know about this?"

"Absolutely not. He needed plausible deniability."

"What about Sam?"

"No, ma'am. Just you. And I'm sure you're aware of your ethical obligations as a lawyer. You have to keep this to yourself."

"And you must be aware that I am not allowed to put you on the stand if I know you're going to commit perjury."

"Then *you* can't put me on the stand." He leaned forward in his chair.

"You just played me."

"I have no idea what you mean."

"You knew that once you told me that you forged documents, I couldn't willingly put you on the stand. I have no way of knowing whether you're telling the truth or not. But the bottom line is you don't want to testify. But even if we don't call you in our case in chief, they're going to call you in their case. You'll be on the stand either way."

He smiled widely. "You know, I really like you, Hope. I'd like you to consider being my personal attorney."

She wanted to immediately shoot him down. But before she opened her mouth, it occurred to her that she shouldn't just reject his proposition. If she worked more closely with him, she could find out more intel on his businesses. "I can't be your attorney if you're dishonest with me. Trust is key to the relationship."

He nodded.

"So why don't we start with the Cyber Future Chip and go from there."

"I really have no idea about that. If I did, I would tell you."

He continued to look her directly in the eyes and lie. This was dangerous. She had to hold back her fear and keep putting on this act. "All right. You're saying you have no idea why it is they think that Wakefield stole the chip?"

"I have no idea. I think they are just trying to stir up trouble."

"With all due respect, sending a hit man after me multiple times is much more than trouble."

He grinned. "There's that fire I like to see."

"Back to our immediate problem. You know you'll still have to testify. They're going to call you as a witness in their case."

"I understand that."

"And you're going to lie." As she said the words it was all becoming clear what his game was. "You're going to lie when then they examine you."

"I obviously won't tell the truth. It's up to you whether you question me."

"You're putting me in an impossible position. You do realize, though, that at this point, Wakefield is our firms' client. Not you in your personal capacity."

"I do. But you realize that it's in Wakefield's best interest if I lie."

Her head began to pound. What should she do? She had to keep the bigger picture in mind. There was an active FBI investigation into this man. If she could aid in that investigation, then she should. But she had her ethical responsibilities, too. "This is all a lot to take in."

"I understand. And I can tell from getting to know you that you aren't really the type of person to want to work with a man like me. But we can make a good team, Hope. If you just give me a chance. Just think of what bringing me in as a client would do for your partnership chances. And I'd demand that you get full credit for all my business."

"Thank, Carlos. I'd like to think it over." She wanted to add something though. "I appreciate you believing in me."

He smiled obviously feeling like he scored a victory. If only he knew the truth.

"You know how to find me, Hope. And also consider letting me provide you with additional security."

"Thank you, Carlos."

He walked out of her office, and she let out a deep breath. Sitting in a state of disbelief. She had not been expecting that. She'd reviewed all the documents in the case—multiple times. Now to find out that Nola had forged the key documents made her sick. This guy was even more unscrupulous than she initially believed.

Nola put on such a good act, though. She'd enjoyed working with him. He'd been a great resource at Wakefield for her. And yeah, he was stubborn, but most all of the business guys she dealt with were like that. It was just how they were. He'd always been nice to her and treated her with respect. Now she couldn't help but wonder how dangerous this man really was. Was he capable of truly heinous acts or was he just a white collar criminal?

He was lying about the Cyber Future Chip. What else was he lying about? A chill shot through her remembering that look in his eyes. Totally devoid of emotion. He was able to lie with a straight face. That made him even more dangerous.

A light knock on the door was followed by Gabe's head peeking in.

She motioned for him to come into the office.

"Something's wrong," he said.

"I don't even know where to begin."

"Just start at the beginning. The last thing I heard was him telling you that you needed to know something before he took the stand."

She looked down at her hands which were currently balled up and tried to relax. This was Gabe. He was on her side. "Well, let's see." She paused. "He informed me that he forged documents. That Wakefield did actually breach the contract, but he forged documents showing Wakefield made the payment. I suspect that he diverted those funds to promote his criminal enterprise."

Gabe's dark eyes widened. "I must admit, I didn't see that coming."

"Me neither. I reviewed those documents personally. I'm familiar with each one of them. I had no way of knowing that they weren't real. I'm still trying to wrap my head around it."

"What happened when he told you that?"

"We had a discussion about whether he was going to take the stand as part of our case as one of our affirmative witnesses. He knew that I'd be put in a very difficult situation knowing that. As a lawyer, if you know your client is going to perjure themselves, you can't put them on the stand. Now, you have to be pretty certain about their perjurious intent. But still." She sighed and shook her head. "He's going to lie on the stand because Cyber Future's going to call him as a witness."

"What are you supposed to do about that?"

"I don't know, but there's more."

"Okay."

She stood up and walked around the front of the desk. "He wants me to be his personal attorney."

"He what?" Gabe walked over to her and grabbed her hands. "Are you serious?"

"Yes."

"What did you say?" He dropped her hands, and she paced back and forth.

"I told him I was flattered and that I'd think about it. Of course, I wanted to tell him no way, but I had the sense to realize that this might be a golden opportunity for the investigation."

"You're brilliant, Hope. Truly brilliant. You are right. This could be just what we needed to crack the case."

"So we left it with me getting back to him. He also lied to me about the Cyber Future Chip. He still claims he knows absolutely nothing about it."

"Which is why we need to find that drive at the company in the files you sent and prove otherwise."

"I know."

"But we can't mess up this opportunity with Nola. You could have unprecedented access."

"I'm in a very precarious position. Wakefield is my client right now. I need to figure out what I'm obligated to do with what Nola told me."

"Won't everyone figure out something is up if you all of a sudden say you aren't going to put him on the stand?"

"Or worse, that I don't examine him after they put him on in their case."

"I know you're not going to like this."

"Uh oh. What have you got brewing in that mind of yours?"

He smiled at her as she sat back down in the desk chair.

"You don't have to do the exam. Make Sam do it."

"That means I have to keep this information from him."

"Given the security threat involved in the ongoing FBI investigation, it's more than justified. And as an FBI agent, I'm asking you to do just that."

"I was afraid you were going to say that. This isn't easy for me."

"I know, Hope. But you're doing the right thing here. Once this is over, you can go back to your regular life in New York practicing law without these threats and dangers. For now, though, I really need you to let me know if you think you can handle taking on Nola."

"I have no problem taking him on. But I feel very uncomfortable saying yes to representing him. I think it's a pretty questionable line in the sand. Can I just string him along for a little while? Say I want to learn more about his businesses before I accept?"

"That's a perfect idea. You would be basically working as a confidential informant for the FBI."

She bit her bottom lip and carefully considered what he was saying. She was already in so deep there was probably no way out. Not to mention the fact that some organized crime group probably wanted her dead. "Okay," she said reluctantly. "For now we need to get to Wakefield and start looking for that chip. We can just say that I need to review certain files.

"Let's go."

***

Hope had gotten sidetracked with some legal work that had to be completed before the close of business. So it wasn't until early evening when they stood in a conference room at Wakefield filled with dozens and dozens of banker's boxes of documents when Gabe looked over at her.

Gabe was asking so much of her. And she was asking a lot of herself, too. In addition to the very real personal danger she was facing, now to take on the role as a confidential informant might prove to be too much for her. Could she take the stress without crumbling? She didn't see any alternative, so she she'd just have to keep her head up and push forward. There was no turning back now.

"So are we just going to look through each box?" he asked.

"Well, I've got an idea of a few boxes to start with based on how our records department labeled the files. Why don't you start looking through these?" She pointed to a stack of boxes on the floor. "And I'll look through these."

"And it most likely won't be in there loose, right?"

"Exactly, most likely my secretary or the records department would have placed the jump drive into an envelope and put it in a folder and labeled it as client files."

"I'm on it." He opened the first box and started searching.

"Don't go too fast. Sometimes things get stuck together or fall in the bottom of a folder."

"I'll be careful."

An hour later, neither one of them had found anything.

"This just doesn't make sense," she said.

"Or it makes perfect sense. Nola knew the general process for the files, and he got here before us."

She kicked one of the boxes showing her frustration. He walked over to her and put his hand on her shoulder. "It's going to be okay, Hope."

"That's easy for you to say. You aren't the one they want dead." She stood with her hand on her hip.

"Would Nola keep it himself or hand it off to someone else?"

"Your guess is as good as mine," she said. "We don't even know who else he is working with."

"You're right. And that can be one of the first things you find out."

"You really think this plan will work?"

"It's our best chance. He's really taking a liking to you. You've proven to be tough, resilient, and savvy. Add ambition and desire to rise to the top to that mix and he probably sees you as someone who could be very valuable to him."

"Is that how you see me? Ambitious? What else?" She narrowed her eyes.

"Wait, I meant all that as a compliment."

"I'm just a big city lawyer and social climber."

"Whoa, now, where is all this coming from?"

She sighed and sat down on one of the boxes. "I'm sorry. I'm feeling frustrated." She pulled her hair back and twisted it up into a bun only to have it fall a second later.

"I really didn't mean any disrespect."

"I know. But you're right. I am obsessed with my career. I need that stability. I need to feel like I'll be okay all on my own. I won't worry about money or security."

"You mentioned your childhood. I can imagine that really has shaped your feelings on your work."

"When I was growing up, I told myself that I would work tirelessly to make sure I never went to bed hungry again. If that meant going to school and studying around the clock so I could have a stable well-paying job, then so be it."

"How did you pay for school?"

"Loans. I got a lot of public funding since I was so poor. But I also had to take out some private loans for law school. I'm still paying them off, but it was totally worth it."

"Where are your parents now?'

"They're both dead. My dad had a heart attack and my mom had problems with alcohol. It was really tough."

"You've been through a lot in your life, Hope."

"I don't want your pity, Gabe. Just your respect."

"I'm not pitying you. And you earned my respect more quickly than most. It's not an easy task. I just can't help but think how different our lives were growing up."

"I'm sure they were. But I'm here now, and we need to figure a way out of this before it's too late."

"I've got an idea. Why don't we get out of here? I can take you over and show you my house. Fix us some dinner there and you can meet my better half."

"Huh?"

"My Labrador Zeke. Caleb dropped him off a little bit ago because I wanted to run home and see him and get some more stuff from my house."

She couldn't help but laugh.

"You have to eat. And I'll feel safer at my place than out somewhere in town."

She was tired and hungry so she didn't argue with him. It would also be nice to meet his dog. Maybe that would cheer her up.

As she buckled her seatbelt, she looked in the rearview mirror. No sign of anyone. She was no longer in a state of paranoia. Her fears were justified. "How far away do you live?"

"I'm just a couple miles out."

"So further away from town?"

"Yeah. I like it out there. It's still not far away from everything. But it gives me my privacy, and I have a little bit of land for Zeke to run and play."

"I guess in a small town it can get frustrating with everyone knowing your business."

"That's true. I've gotten used to a lot of it, but it can still be difficult. So I wouldn't move closer into town if you paid me."

A few minutes later, they pulled up in front of a large cabin. "Wow. It looks like a country cabin out of a magazine."

"Can I take that as a compliment?"

"Yes. It's gorgeous."

"Thanks. It's my design. I can't take credit for building it, but it was definitely my vision. Turned out exactly how I wanted it to."

"Kinda big for you, though."

"Well I built it in mind that it would house my family someday."

"Oh," she said silently. Why did it bother her that he said that? She had no claim on him. They were friends. Partners. Nothing more. Like she would ever live in this cabin in the country. Like he would ever want a woman like her.

She stepped out of the car and heard loud barking.

"That's Zeke welcoming us. Come on." He took her by the hand and guided her up the front porch steps.

Two rocking chairs and a swing sat on the well-lit porch.

Gabe unlocked the door and a huge black fluff of a dog jumped around at his feet.

"Hey, big guy." Gabe squatted down and loved all over his dog. Zeke's tail wagged quickly, and he let out a few excited barks. But then Hope realized the moment when Zeke focused in on her. The newcomer.

"Don't worry," Gabe said. "He's huge, but he's friendly. Or at least when I tell him to be."

She couldn't help but smile as Zeke ran over to her and started licking her hand. His dark fur felt so soft and warm under her touch. "He's beautiful."

"No, beautiful is for ladies. He's handsome." He laughed.

"All right. Zeke, you are very handsome." His tail wagged faster and faster. Then he ran to the other room and came back with a tennis ball.

"Oh no, Zeke. Let Hope get settled in before you start harassing her to play fetch with you in the yard."

Zeke stood undeterred, with his tail held high and the yellow tennis ball firmly entrenched in his mouth. "It's okay, Gabe. I'd love to play with him."

"If you're sure. I'll start dinner then. Let me show you out back. I've got a fenced in area for him."

He guided her out the back door where there was a screened in porch. "I love this porch," she said.

"Yeah, it's great. Especially nice to sit outside and not be bothered by the mosquitos. Zeke hangs out here a lot."

She looked and saw a huge blue dog bed in the corner filled with bones and stuffed toys.

He opened the door and she walked down the steps with Zeke right beside her.

"I'll turn on the floodlights." He reached for the lights inside the porch and then the backyard was fully illuminated. Zeke barked impatiently. "Have fun, and don't let him wear you out. He could go all night. Just come in when you get tired."

She took a tennis ball and threw it hard and Zeke took off running. While he retrieved it, she inhaled a deep breath, letting the mild air fill her lungs. This was the first moment of true peace she'd felt since she arrived in Maxwell.

Zeke came running full out toward her, with ball firmly in his mouth. She thought for a moment he was going to mow her over, but he stopped promptly in front of her dropping the ball at her feet. Then he let out a single bark. "I get it, Zeke." She laughed to herself and threw the ball until her arm felt like it was about to fall off.

"All right, Zekester. You've worn me out. Let's go inside and relax."

He listened to her although she could tell that he would play as long as she was out there. "Good boy."

When she walked back into the house, the smell of tomato sauce filled the air.

"Hey, I thought I was going to have to go out there and save you." He stood at the stove stirring the sauce.

"It was fun." She paused. "And that smell is amazing."

"Just some spaghetti. Easy enough."

"Well regardless, it smells wonderful. Thanks for cooking."

"Just needs a little time to simmer. Then we can eat. You're also going to be happy because I have bread from the bakery downtown."

Her stomach rumbled at the thought. Then she heard the front door open and shut.

"Dear, you're cooking." A female voice rang out.

Uh oh, she thought. She turned expecting to see a young female. But instead the voice belonged to an older lady with short silver hair. She wore a periwinkle scarf over her navy sweater.

"Oh, Gabe." The woman's eyes widened. "I'm so sorry. I didn't know you had company."

Gabe walked over to the lady. "No problem, mom." He grabbed her into a big bear hug. "I'm always happy to see you. Mom, this is Hope Finch. She's one of the lawyers in town working on the Wakefield trial."

"Yes. I've heard all about that." She walked over and extended her hand. "I'm Ruth. We're so glad to have you in Maxwell. This trial is the talk of the town."

"Thank you for having me."

"And how did you meet Gabe?"

Before she could answer, he piped up. "I'm doing some consulting for Wakefield."

"That's nice. You work too much, though, son. You need time to yourself." Her blue eyes narrowed at him accusingly. "Have you lost a few pounds?"

"No, Mom. I haven't."

She turned toward Hope. "I have to keep my eye on this one. He needs someone watching out for him. So consumed in his work."

"Mom, do we really need to have this discussion right now?" he asked.

She laughed. "I'll let you two get to dinner. If you need anything at all while you're in town, Hope, just let me know."

Before either one of them could say anything, Ruth was patting Zeke's head and then walking out the door.

"I'm sorry about that," he said. "My mom can be a bit invasive—in the nicest way possible. And she has no problem jumping to conclusions." He filled up a dog food bowl and set it down for Zeke.

"You mean thinking that there's something between you and me?"

"Yeah, and I can't blame her. She knows I rarely bring women over to my house."

"And why is that?"

"I like my privacy. I like my space. It's just better that way."

"I understand. I'm the same way."

"The invitation stands about going to church, though."

"I just don't know if I'm up for that."

"If you change your mind, just let me know." He turned around back to the stove. "It's time to eat. Sit down and I'll bring you a plate."

"You're doing well in the kitchen to be a bachelor."

He laughed loudly as he sat down the huge plate of piping hot spaghetti in front of her with a large roll on the side. "I have to be good in kitchen *because* I'm a bachelor." He paused. "You mind if I say grace before we eat?"

"No, go ahead." This was all a bit unfamiliar territory to her, and yet it felt so comfortable for him.

He said a quick prayer and then picked up his own fork. She looked down and saw that Zeke was positioned right by her side.

"Just ignore him. He knows he'll get in trouble if he begs too much."

"Can't I give him a bite?"

"No. You'll create a monster, believe me. Labs are hyper food driven. It's taking all his discipline to sit there right now and not whine. You saw me feed him. He's not hungry. He just can't help himself."

"I'm a softie when it comes to animals."

He smiled. "I can see that. Another side of you that's unexpected."

"Thanks, I think." She took another bite and enjoyed the warm tomato sauce. "This is delicious."

"I'm glad you like it."

When they finished she got up to clear the table. "You cooked, the least I can do is clean up."

"All right. No complaints there."

Zeke started barking and ran to the back door.

"What's gotten into him?" she asked.

Zeke's barking only got louder and louder.

She looked out the back window and couldn't see anything but darkness.

Gabe pulled out his gun from his holster. "I don't know what's happening. But it's not like Zeke to bark for no reason. Stay inside and lock the door behind me. Do not let anyone in. You hear me?"

"Yes," she said. But he was already out the door. She locked it behind him, and Zeke stood at attention by her side.

A gunshot rang out, and she instinctively crouched down. Zeke barked and nudged her hand. "What should we do?" she asked him. Yes, she was talking to a dog. But he seemed insistent that they move. To where, she didn't know.

Staying low to the ground she started making her way toward the interior bathroom. Yes, get away from all the windows, she thought. Another shot rang out loudly. She desperately hoped that Gabe wasn't hurt. Or worse.

She grabbed onto Zeke and waited. After a few minutes with no sound, she wondered what she should do. What if Gabe was injured and needed medical attention? She knew CPR and basic first aid.

Deciding that she wasn't going to hide any longer, she slowly turned the bathroom doorknob and it opened with a creek. Taking a deep breath, she stayed crouched down and scooted into the hallway.

Zeke took off running. Oh no. She couldn't let him get hurt. She stood up and ran after him. He was waiting at the porch door. Yeah, Gabe had specifically told her not to open it, but she had no choice. Looking around the kitchen, she found a large knife. Grabbing it tightly in her right hand, she twisted the lock with her left and opened the door.

Silence. Complete silence. Zeke brushed by her and starting running. She'd have to rely on him to find Gabe.

She was a few steps behind Zeke, but she couldn't see anything. Chills shot down her arms as she envisioned the worst case scenarios. Gabe was injured or dead and the shooter was now going to come after her.

Zeke started barking loudly, and she ran over quickly to where she heard him. Then she heard a grunt.

"Gabe, are you okay?" She couldn't see much to tell how he was doing.

"Yeah. It's just a superficial gunshot wound."

"You've been shot! I need to call 9-1-1."

"I'll be fine, Hope. It's more of a graze."

"Then why were you on the ground?"

"I was waiting. I got off a few shots, but wasn't sure if I hit the target."

"I haven't seen anyone. I only heard the shots."

"You shouldn't be out here. It's too dangerous."

"I couldn't abandon you," she said softly.

"You're a good partner." He stood up and they walked back toward the house.

That's when she heard the loan moaning sound. "Someone's there," she whispered.

"Run inside and turn the flood lights back on. Wait on me there."

Knowing it probably wasn't the time to argue, she did as instructed. She paced around the kitchen waiting. The sound of sirens soon filled the air. Gabe walked back inside with Zeke by his side.

"What happened?"

"Looks like I shot the guy in the shoulder. He's in pain, but it's not life threatening."

"Were you able to question him?"

A loud knock at the door interrupted the conversation.

"That has to be Caleb." Gabe walked to the front door and let in Caleb and a few uniformed officers. "There's a guy in the back cuffed to the porch railing." The uniformed officers walked out the back door.

"What happened here?" Caleb asked. He frowned as he looked back and forth at both of them.

She nodded toward Gabe to go ahead.

"We were finishing dinner and Zeke started barking. He was very persistent, not like his normal self. I knew someone had to be outside. So I went out back to check it out. The perpetrator fired the first shot at me. Missed. I returned fire. We did that three times. My final shot got him. I was flying blind because I couldn't see him."

Caleb turned to her. "And what about you?"

"Well I hid in the bathroom with Zeke. But then I when things got quiet, I started getting worried about Gabe being hurt. I had heard the gunshots. So I decided I needed to check it out. I went outside with Zeke and that's how Zeke led me to Gabe. Then we found the intruder."

Caleb paced around the living room. "We're missing something here. Hope, they want you badly enough to kidnap you or kill you. I can't help but think you have to have something they want that goes beyond the allegedly stolen chip."

"Like what?" she asked. Her mind turned cartwheels trying to ascertain why they thought she was so valuable.

"What if it's about the Wakefield Chip too?" Gabe asked.

"How do you figure that?" Caleb asked.

"Hope." Gabe looked at her. "Do you have any special knowledge about the Wakefield Chip?"

"I'm very familiar with the patent. But anyone with a patent background could understand it. So it's not like a secret formula if that's what you're asking."

"What about Cyber Future itself? Were you exposed to anything about them that you could now use against them in this litigation or in some future litigation? Anything in the documents?"

"You realize this is a total shot in the dark, right?" she asked. "We're just guessing."

"Wait. When you said patents it got me thinking." Gabe paused. "What if they think you have the knowledge about the chip? Not just the chip itself but the ability to recreate it."

She shuddered thinking about those implications. "That would be a problem."

Caleb nodded. "I think Gabe's onto something. That would explain why they would get desperate and just try to kill you if they couldn't question you."

She clenched her fists. "How could this chip be so important that they would be willing to kill me?"

"That is a missing factor. But what if it's tied to something other than just general security applications. Think outside the box, like it could be for some sort of military purpose, or some type of cyber warfare."

"Pure speculation," Caleb said.

"But you see where I'm going."

"And as long as they think I know something, I'll never be safe again." How was she going to get out of this? "What do I do?"

"We need to find out who is behind this at Cyber Future. That would give us a big indication of what they're after. What industry they're tied up with. Or if we're totally off base, we'll need to figure that out too."

"But that doesn't change the fact that I know absolutely nothing about the Cyber Future Chip. The only person we know who does is Carlos Nola."

"Hope's right. It may be time to get more aggressive with Nola," Caleb said.

"But we have the larger investigation to keep in consideration," Gabe replied. "We can't forget about that."

"Are you seriously worried about that right now?" She was quickly losing her temper.

"Nola's network is spreading in this town. If we act too soon against him, we may lose our opportunity. That's all I'm saying. To put too much heat on Nola risks any strategic advantage we have at this point."

"I'm the target of multiple hit men and enemy number one of a corporation probably backed by organized crime and you're worried about a little bit of petty crime in Maxwell. Crime that you really have no solid evidence even tying Nola to?" She shifted her weight and leaned up against the wall. "This is unbelievable."

Caleb eyed them both warily. "I'm going to go check on the suspect." Caleb walked out the porch door.

Gabe walked over and stood directly in front of her. He placed his hands on her shoulders. "I'm sorry, Hope. I wasn't trying to upset you."

"Don't apologize for upsetting me. Apologize for having a bad idea."

He took a step closer. "Hope, I care about you. You have to know that I will do everything in my power to protect you."

"You want to have it both ways. Have your original Nola investigation neatly tied up like a bow, and keep me safe. And I'm telling you, that's probably not possible. If you have to choose, honestly right now, I'm not sure how you would decide."

He leaned down and pressed his lips gently to hers. Before she could really register what had happened, he pulled back. Then he smiled and grabbed onto her hands. "Hope, have no doubts about what my decision would be."

He dropped her hands and walked out the porch door. She stood in shock. What had just happened?

CHAPTER NINE

Had Gabe really kissed Hope? What in the world was he thinking? One moment she was arguing with him, telling him what a bad decision he was making. The next, he kissed her.

He'd gone over in his head why they would never work. Over and over again. She was all about the city. All about her high power career. She didn't have the same background as he did.

But at the end of the day, was he willing to put that aside? And shouldn't he cut her some slack? She'd had a rough life. His seemed like a cakewalk in comparison. Granted, his family didn't have a lot of money, but he always had everything he needed growing up. There was always food on the table, new clothes, and even some small luxuries now and again.

It wasn't fair for him to impose his life experience on hers. It was up to him to lead by example. And instead, he'd pushed an idea that was probably pigheaded. He'd let his feelings for Nola get in the way of his better judgment. She'd called him out on it. And she was right.

Of course Hope was more important than his investigation. He didn't know how to handle the fact that he was developing strong feelings for her. Not just as her protector, but as someone who really wanted to be with her. To know more about her. And to keep her safe. Not just safe from Cyber Future or Nola, but safe from all the harms in the world.

He shook his head as if that would clear his thoughts. She'd gone back to the inn last night and not said a word on the drive over. Caleb had taken Zeke back with him to dog sit, and Gabe stayed next door to Hope at the inn.

He barely slept at all, and was ready for a hot cup of coffee. Was Hope even awake? He looked at the clock that had just turned to seven a.m.

He lightly knocked on her door. If she was still asleep, chances were she wouldn't hear him. But in a minute, the door opened ever so slightly. There she was. Giving him the eye. He was still in trouble. Now he had to make it up to her.

"I was thinking we could grab a good breakfast at the diner if you were up for it?"

She looked at him for a moment. Then she nodded. "I need a few minutes to get ready."

"How long is a few? Few in women terms can mean a lot of different things."

"Can I have half an hour? I'd like to take a hot shower to try to wake up. I didn't sleep very well last night."

"Of course. I'll be back in thirty minutes to get you."

She didn't respond, but shut the door. He was in trouble. He didn't know whether she was upset about his investigation, the kiss, or both.

He took a deep breath before he knocked on her door thirty minutes later. Hoping she'd be in a better mood. He knew from the moment the door opened that he was still in trouble. Deep trouble.

They walked in silence out to his car. He couldn't take it anymore so he spoke. "You're obviously upset with me. We need to talk about it so we can move forward."

"I don't think that's necessary."

He pulled into Pa's parking lot but kept the car running. He looked over at her, but she didn't make eye contact. "Was it the kiss? If I overstepped, I apologize."

"You really think that's what I'm upset about?" She turned and looked at him. Then she laughed. "You are so clueless."

"Then maybe I do need you to spell it out for me."

"This isn't about the kiss. It was just a kiss." She shook her head. "I'm upset about your obsession with Nola and how you've let that cloud your judgment."

He reached out and touched her arm. "My judgment is not clouded."

"I don't want to argue. Let's go get breakfast. I could really use some coffee."

Deciding it was better to let it go for now, he simply nodded and got out of the car. He had to make her believe in him again. That he wouldn't sell her out for his investigation. Because quite simply—he wouldn't.

After they ordered breakfast, they drank their coffee. He gave her a minute to enjoy it before he started talking again.

"Hope, you're the priority. Your safety. Not Nola. Not my investigation."

"And how do I know that you really mean that?" She took a sip of coffee and then put her big mug back down in front of her. "From the beginning you've been focused on your investigation. And I get that. That's your job. But things have gone way beyond threats."

He reached out and grabbed her hands. "I know. Why do you think I am not letting you leave my side? I get that this is dangerous, and that you're a target. I'll admit, I am anxious to get Nola, but I'm not going to do anything to put you in more danger. If that means blowing the Nola investigation, I am more than okay with that."

"That isn't what it sounded like last night?"

"That was an FBI agent gut reaction. Once you pointed out how wrong I was, I realized you were right. So let this be my apology."

She smiled. "Accepted. But how do we move onto the trial? What do I need to do?"

Mags walked over to the table and put their food in front of them. He wondered if the stress had caused Hope to order the large southern style breakfast complete with bacon, biscuits and gravy, and eggs.

"I think you know that you need more information from Nola. Say you're seriously considering his offer to work as his private attorney but some of the security issues are making you nervous. You need to fully comprehend what type of risk you face. I think if you go with that, you'll come away with something possibly valuable."

She sighed. "I can't believe he's going to lie on the stand. You hear about clients doing that, but I've never experienced anything like it firsthand."

"When we get done here, you should give him a call. Ask for a meeting."

She looked down and then back up again. "I didn't ask for any of this."

"I'm on your side, Hope. We're going to get through this as a team."

"And what are you going to be doing when I'm meeting with Nola?" She took a bite of eggs and waited for him to answer.

"I won't be far. Don't worry about that."

"Any good meeting place suggestions?"

"Let him pick. You want him as comfortable as he can be."

She frowned. "What about my comfort level?"

"You've made it this far. This meeting will be a piece of cake. You've got this."

"I'm glad you're so confident."

"Make the call."

"Now?"

"Why not. And try to set something up as soon as possible. But don't sound too desperate."

She laughed and leaned forward in the booth. "You sure are bossy. This is my issue. I'll deal with it my way."

"Fair enough. But please make the call."

She grabbed her cell out of her purse and held it up as if trying to make a point. She had a stubborn streak that matched his own. But it was also cute.

"Hi, Carlos, how are you?"

He sat there only hearing her side of the conversation. He had to give it to her. She was working him over like a pro. But in a totally sweet and non-threatening way. She was so valuable to the investigation because Nola would never see her coming.

A satisfied smile spread across her face, and he knew that she had him. She said goodbye and put her phone back in her purse.

"And that's how it's done, Mr. Security Specialist."

He laughed. "Good job."

"I'm meeting him at the Maxwell public library in half an hour."

"Then let's finish up so you can get going."

* * *

Hope hadn't been completely honest with Gabe. Yeah, she had been mad about his Nola investigation. But the kiss wasn't just a kiss. She'd only said that to try to save face.

Sitting at the table in the Maxwell public library, she tried to regain her composure now that she was out of Gabe's presence. Why did he unnerve her so? Had she allowed herself to develop feelings for him?

She'd promised herself after the Barry disaster that she would not let another man into her life emotionally for a long time—if ever. And she'd gone and done just that.

Drumming her fingers nervously on the table, she needed to get a grip and focus on the life and death problem facing her instead of acting like a high school girl with a crush. Carlos Nola had fooled her initially, but her eyes were now open. Beyond that smooth and professional exterior was most likely a man involved in criminal activity. Activity that could get her killed.

A hand on her shoulder caused her to jump.

"Oh, I'm sorry, Hope. I didn't mean to startle you," Nola said.

"I'm probably a bit on edge given everything that's been happening."

He took a seat beside her. "Have you given any more thought to my business proposition?"

She nodded. "I have. But I'd like some more information before we proceed."

He looked around as if making sure that there was no one milling around that could hear their conversation. "What would you like to know?"

Leaning in closer to him, she made direct eye contact. His expression was all business. "I think you know how dangerous this situation has become for me personally. And I also know that you're very guarded with your information and who you let inside your circle. Before I can fully entertain your offer, I need straight answers. I need to know the truth about the Cyber Future Chip to start with. And your role in all of that."

"What exactly do you want to know?"

"You stole the chip, right? When you told me you had nothing to do with it that was a lie."

He didn't respond.

"All right. I take your silence as acquiescence." She paused, giving him the opportunity to deny it, but he didn't. "So what I need to know is what is on that chip. And who is behind the attacks against me?"

He twisted his scarf around his fingers. "I can't exactly answer that."

"Why not?"

"I'm still trying to figure out both of those myself."

"But if you stole the chip, you have to know what's on it."

"You're making an assumption there."

"I'm tired of your riddles. This is important, so stop giving me the runaround." It was time for her to play hardball. No more nice Hope. She needed to convince Nola that she was tough enough to run with him. "If that's all you're going to tell me, then this conversation is over." She stood up from her chair. He grabbed her arm. "No, please wait."

"Then start talking."

"This conversation never happened. If you repeat anything I say, I'll deny it. Understood?"

"Go ahead."

"I don't know what is on the chip. It's encrypted and I hadn't been able to break the encryption. I don't trust many of my normal sources because I know that it has to be ultra-sensitive. I was still in search for someone who has the skills and can be trusted. But then everything changed."

"What do you mean?"

"The chip was stolen. I had it removed from your firm and then secured in my office at Wakefield. But someone took it."

"Is there an organized crime connection here, Carlos?"

"To Cyber Future, yes. A faction of an organized crime group in California. Loosely connected to one of the most powerful Asian mafia groups in the U.S."

She sat processing this information. Gabe's theory had been right. This was all connected to organized crime groups. "And you—what group are you connected with?"

"What makes you think I am?" He raised an eyebrow.

"C'mon, Carlos. Don't even try to deny it."

"I'm not technically working with anyone. But I've worked with various groups before when the need arose. But the people I work with are not friends of this California group. That I can say for sure."

"And how can you ensure my protection?"

"I have professional security staff who are up for the job. Much better than that small town guy Lee is relying on."

"If it weren't for that small town guy, I'd already be dead."

"I get that, but I'm saying I can do better. A lot better. But I need to know you'll be all in. Because once you're in, you're in for good."

She tried to hold back a chill. "I'll give you my final answer after the trial is over. That has to be my immediate focus."

"And I assume you won't be putting me on the stand? Or at least you won't be questioning me?"

"And I think you know the answer to that." She needed to get out of the library now. She felt like the world was starting to close in around her. She was literally boxed in. Everywhere she looked there was danger—both internally and externally. "I need to go. I've got a lot of trial prep to do."

"We'll talk soon."

She stood up and walked quickly out of the library. Searching for the cool air outside. The reality of the situation hit her. She was stuck in the middle of a war between rival organized crime groups. Her life was in the balance.

Turning and looking over her shoulder, a sense of paranoia overtook her. Gabe had to be close by, right? Shaking off a feeling of dread, she started walking to the law firm.

She'd reached the town square when Gabe appeared seemingly out of nowhere falling into step with her.

"You scared me," she said. "Where did you come from?"

"I told you I wouldn't be far. I had eyes on you the entire time." He put his arm around her and ushered her to the front door of the firm.

"Let's talk in my office."

The Trent Law Firm wouldn't normally be open on the weekend but given the trial started on Monday, there was a buzz of activity. Mainly the staff trying to prepare the final trial exhibits and make Sam's changes to his power point presentation for opening statement.

In her office with the door shut, she took a deep breath. "Your suspicions were right. Cyber Future is working with an organized crime group in California with ties to one of the strongest Asian mafia groups in the area. Nola wouldn't admit which group he was associated with. He would only say that he'd worked with several groups in the past, and the one he is currently working with is an enemy of this California group."

"But no names on either of the groups?"

"No. But he made it seem like the California group may be an offshoot or something."

"Highly plausible that the group Cyber Future is working with is funded by the mafia. Like everything else, organized crime is having to shift and adapt to the advances in technology. Maybe something about Cyber Future piqued their interest and they started working together."

"It's a very lucrative business. I could see how organized crime groups would want to make sure they had their hands in part of the business."

"Yeah, the intellectual property value alone I'm sure is staggering. But enough to put a persistent hit out on you for? I'm not buying it. There was something on that drive that goes beyond just the Cyber Future Chip. Or the Wakefield Chip for that matter."

"All of that is not the biggest piece of information I got from this meeting."

"What else did you learn?"

She looked at him. "Nola said he was trying to have the chip decrypted. He had it stored in his office at Wakefield. Someone stole it."

"Wow. So we have no idea who actually has this chip now."

"Exactly. Which means I'm going to be in danger. There's no way to fix the problem if we don't understand what is on that chip."

"I'll reach out to my FBI contacts and see if there's anything they could come up with. In the meantime, I'll keep you safe and you can get ready for your trial. I know this means a lot to you. This trial. And as messed up as things have become, I want you to at least enjoy a shred of this experience."

"That means a lot to me to hear you say that, Gabe." She didn't want to say it but she had to. "If things were different, Gabe, I could really see wanting to spend more time with you."

"You're talking about the distance?"

"That's the start. But look at us. You belong here in this town, and I belong in New York at my firm. Our backgrounds couldn't be more different."

"Our backgrounds and our cities don't define us, Hope." He walked around to where she was sitting behind the desk and squatted down beside her. He grabbed her hands and looked up at her.

"I think you and I both know that there is a huge gulf between us."

He squeezed her hands. "There doesn't have to be."

She shook her head. "No, it just can't be." Pulling away she stood and walked to the other side of the office. Turning to face him, she felt her face redden. "Please let's just focus on the work."

He frowned. "All right. For now."

∗∗∗

Gabe had made up his mind. He had developed true feelings for Hope. He wasn't going to let her slip through his fingers. For now, though, he had her safety to worry about.

The sun had just come up on Monday morning, and he was at Hope's hotel room picking her up. He had hot breakfast sandwiches in his hands. They would eat and then head to the courthouse. The plan was settled on the night before. Gabe would be in charge of Hope. The police detail led by Caleb would provide security for Lee and Nola. The main contingent was meeting at the law office and going en masse to the courthouse. Everyone thought it would be better and safer for Gabe and Hope to arrive separately.

"Hey," she said. She opened the door wearing a black power suit with a red blouse. She surely didn't seem like a fearful woman. No, she looked determined.

"I've got us breakfast and coffee." He held out the drink container holding two cups of coffee. She took it and placed it on her small table.

"Nothing like a greasy biscuit to really get you going." He chuckled.

"I've probably already gained ten pounds from being here. I was thankful my suit fit." She laughed. "I got an email from Sam. He's already at the firm and waiting on everyone to arrive."

"So this is it."

"Yeah. Although when I envisioned the first day of trial, this was not what I had in mind. Having a security escort never crossed my mind." She took a bite of the biscuit.

A little crumb lingered on the side of her mouth. He couldn't help himself. He reached out and brushed it away.

"Sorry, you had a crumb."

She smiled. "Thanks for trying to put me at ease. I know what you're doing. But you don't have to worry about me. My head is in the game. I promise."

"I never doubted that. Hope, you're one of the strongest people I've ever met." He reached over and took her hand in his.

"I thought we went over this already, Gabe."

"I can be very persistent." He thought she was going to pull away but she didn't. Instead he thought he saw a mist of tears form in her big brown eyes.

"Don't promise me things, Gabe. In my experience, no one every keeps their promises." She looked down.

"I can tell you've had a lot of heartache in your life. But there are people who won't let you down. I'm one of those people, Hope. If you'll let me in."

She shook her head. "I can't deal with the hurt again. After Barry cheated on me, I just don't know a way back from that. At least not right now. My job is what keeps me grounded. It gives me a purpose."

He gently squeezed her hand. "You're more than just your job. And I completely relate because I often feel the same way. But relationships with other people are really what life is all about."

"And your relationship with God," she said quietly.

"Yes. And I hate seeing you hiding from both out of fear that you're going to be hurt again. I believe you and I were brought together for a reason, Hope. I'm not going to give up on you…or give up on us."

She looked up at him. "No one has ever fought for me, Gabe. Not my parents, not my boyfriends, and not those people who claimed to be my friends."

"I'm here now, and I'm going to fight for you." He leaned in and gently kissed her lips. When he leaned back in his chair, she smiled. A real genuine smile that brought joy to his heart.

"We should finish up and get going," she said.

"Yeah." He might be pushing it with her, but he felt like if he didn't he'd lose his window of opportunity. He had to prove to her that he was different than all the other men she'd dealt with in her life. He wouldn't cut and run, and he certainly wouldn't cheat.

He watched as Hope gathered up her laptop bag and a few file folders.

"I'm ready," she said. With her coffee cup in one hand and folders in the other, she looked the part of power lawyer.

By the time they made the short drive to the courthouse, it was him who was nervous. She looked calm and ready to go. But on the inside, he was a mess of nerves. He checked his sidearm and said a quick prayer for Hope's safety.

He took the key out of the ignition and looked over at her.

"I'm ready," she said. "I'm not going to let all of this ruin my first trial as second chair."

He forced a smile. "Let's get you in the courthouse then."

He'd gotten Caleb to give him special permission to bring his gun into the courthouse. There was no way he was going in there unarmed. The stakes were too high. Getting through the extra security wasn't that big of a deal because they arrived in plenty of time and he was technically part of the security staff.

"Wow," Hope said.

They both looked at the mass of people standing in the main lobby of the Maxwell courthouse.

"I bet it's a combination of those called for jury duty and the many spectators," he said quietly.

"Gabe, this has to be over half the town."

"Don't worry. Stay close to me. I'll get you past the crowd and down to the courtroom." He'd done a security sweep and had run through all operational details yesterday with Caleb. Everyone on the security team was well versed in the small courthouse. All the entrance and exits. Every conference room. Every nook and cranny.

"I'm not worried. I'm excited." She smiled.

He could tell how exciting this was for her. Let her focus on the trial, and he would focus on her.

Thankfully, all the faces in the sea of people were familiar to him. Calming his nerves a bit. He put his hand on her back and guided her to the main courtroom. The building only had two courtrooms and they were using the larger one for this trial.

A police officer stood outside the door. At this point, only the legal teams would be allowed inside until they officially started jury selection.

"Hi, I'm Hope Finch, one of the attorneys for Wakefield."

"Yes, ma'am. I think you're the first on your side to arrive. The lawyers for Cyber Future are already in there."

"Thank you," she said.

She turned to him, fire in her eyes. "I've got this."

CHAPTER TEN

This was her time to shine. Five years of hard work culminating in this one day. The first day of trial. The first day of her acting as second chair. She refused to let any fears or dangers distract her.

She pushed her shoulders back, held her head high, and walked straight up to counsel's table for Wakefield. Setting down her laptop bag, she didn't waste any time opening her belongings and getting the table just how she wanted. Sam was old school and would be taking notes on legal pads. But not her, she was going to using her laptop.

"Well, hello, Hope. We meet again," a male voice said.

She looked up and saw the Cyber Future lawyers from the Jennings Law Firm. All three of them standing in front of her. "Hello, Stanley."

"Hope, you've met Walter before. But I'd like to introduce you to Candice Moser. She'll be working with us for the trial."

"Nice to meet you, Candice." She took her hand, and Candice gave her a strong handshake. Almost too strong. Candice was quite a few inches taller than her with long dark hair and dark eyes. She wore a perfectly tailored navy skirt suit.

"Where's the rest of your crew, Hope?" Walter asked.

"They'll be here soon."

"I heard a rumor that old Harry wasn't going to make it. That it was just going to be you and Sam. And your local counsel, of course, but who are we kidding. Your local lawyer does about as much as ours. Pretty much nothing. I have ours on coffee duty."

"Harry has an arbitration out of the country. But we'll be fine without him."

"No doubt. Well may the best man win."

Hope held her tongue and shifted her attention back to organizing the table. She noticed that Gabe was hanging back behind the bar in the first row of seats behind their table.

She heard loud voices and knew that the rest of her team had to be on its way in. Turning, she saw Sam with Lee on one side and Nola on the other. Followed by Will and Greg. Then a stream of support staff. Taking a deep breath, she knew it was time.

"Sam," she said.

"I see the enemy has already set up camp." His gaze shifted over to where Walter stood.

"Yes. I spoke to them."

"Great. And I see you have our table set up." Sam ushered Lee to the counsel's table. He would serve as the Wakefield corporate representative for trial and would sit with the lawyers. Nola hung back and would sit in the front row. All of this had been carefully considered beforehand. Although it was a no brainer that Lee would want to be the face of the company. He was a legend in Maxwell.

"Sam," she said, looking down at her watch. "We should get settled in. It's almost eight thirty. The judge should be in any moment."

"Yes, yes."

Sam took his seat, with Hope sitting next to him, and Lee right beside her. Greg and Will sat in the chairs right behind the table but still in the bar area. She turned and saw Gabe was seated beside Nola in the front row. Just as planned.

The bailiff stood. "All rise. Court is now in session. The Honorable Judge Masters presiding."

Hope didn't want to miss a second of the action. Judge Masters entered the courtroom from his chambers and walked up to the bench. "Everyone can be seated." He paused.

Judge Masters was in his sixties. A no-nonsense southern judge who had been on the bench for twenty years and had no inclination to step down any time soon. He put on his glasses and looked at both counsel's table.

"I see Cyber Future and Wakefield Corporation are well represented. Just like prior hearings in my courtroom, I expect us to stay on schedule. When I tell you to wrap things up for the day, I mean it. Court will run from eight thirty to five each weekday until we finish. Are there any preliminary issues we need to attend to before we start our jury selection process?"

"No, Your Honor," Walter and Sam both said in unison as they stood.

"Very well then. Bailiff, bring in our first group of potential jurors."

Hope knew jury selection was going to be a much easier task for them than for Cyber Future. They had the home field advantage. Cyber Future's lawyers would have a tough time getting people who didn't have some pro Wakefield bias built in. Thankfully for Wakefield, Judge Masters had denied the transfer of venue motion relying heavily on the contract that Cyber Future signed. Sophisticated companies had big firm lawyers and had to live by the contracts they signed. That was the line in Judge Master's opinion that stuck out to her.

But now her bigger problem was how she was going to handle Nola. At least he wouldn't be the first witness up. Before any of that she had to make it through jury selection. It was going to be a long morning.

By the time for the mid-morning break, Hope was shocked that they'd actually picked a jury. She didn't know what Cyber Future's strategy was, but they didn't even use all of their strikes. It was beyond unorthodox to not remove jurors when they had the ability to. They couldn't possibly be that confident in their case.

She took the much needed break to go to the restroom. Gabe was right behind her.

"I'll just be in the bathroom, can you please give me a few minutes."

"Sure," he said. "I'll just be right down the hall."

Nodding, she was glad to have a minute to herself. Even if it was in the ladies room. After using the restroom, she looked at the mirror and decided she could use a little freshening up. She didn't wear a lot of makeup, but still she wanted to look professional.

One of the other stalls opened and Candice walked out. Then she looked into the other stall. "Just wanted to make sure we were alone," Candice said.

"You know we're not supposed to be talking about the case in the bathroom even if we don't see any jurors in here."

Candice smiled. Then she pulled out a small gun, pointing it directly at Hope.

Hope felt like she was on a free fall and gripped onto the sink. "What are you doing? How did you get a weapon in here?"

"We don't have time for small talk. This is what's going to happen. You're going to walk out of here with me. Anyone asks anything, say we're running to grab coffee. You say a word and I shoot you or someone else."

"You're working for the organized crime group out of California."

"Well you aren't as stupid as you look. I guess not all blondes are dumb. C'mon, let's move. Put a smile on that face before I blow it off." She pushed her toward the door just as another woman walked in.

But what could she do? She couldn't leave that courthouse or she'd be signing her death warrant. It wouldn't surprise her if Candice wasn't even a lawyer. But some hired female assassin.

"Hope, where are you going?" Gabe's voice rang out down the courthouse hallway.

"Don't you dare think about doing anything stupid," Candice said quietly.

"We're just running to get coffee," Hope said.

"Where?"

She blinked quickly a few times. The only thing she knew to do was to try and let him know something was off. "Coffee at Mel's," then she added, "I was just telling Candice they have the best coffee." She was counting on Candice not knowing the area restaurants.

"Great, I'll go with you," he said.

"Not necessary," Candice added. "I'd like a couple of minutes of girl time with Hope."

That did it. Something flashed in Gabe's dark eyes, and before Hope could even react, he had Candice up against the wall. He found her gun and disarmed her quickly. "I don't know who you are, but I'm guessing you're not really a lawyer for Cyber Future. But you are going to be under arrest. You can make a scene or you can go quietly."

"And who are you?"

"Private security. But I'm taking you to the Maxwell police chief."

Candice turned and looked at Hope over her shoulder. "You're going to regret not going with me. I would've killed you quickly. I can't say the same for those that will come after you now."

A shiver went down her arms.

"Enough out of you," Gabe snapped. Then he looked back at Hope. "Stay with us. Until I can get this resolved I don't want you out of my sight."

She nodded and agreed with him. When would this ever stop? She refused to be shut out of the action in the courtroom though. She'd earned second chair, and she was going to fight for it.

Gabe kept Candice close to him, and Hope stayed a step behind the two of them.

Gabe motioned to Caleb with his free hand, and Caleb walked over with a frown on his face.

"What's this?" Caleb asked.

Gabe looked around. He obviously was trying not to make a scene. "This woman attacked Hope. She had a gun. I've got it under my jacket now."

Caleb looked toward Hope and she nodded. "You're going to have to come with me, ma'am."

Candice turned back toward Hope. "You can't stop this. You know too much. Or they think you do. They won't ever leave you alone. Ever. You have no idea what you're up against. These guys won't be able to protect you forever."

"Enough," Caleb said. He guided Candice down the corridor.

"I'm going back into the courtroom. We should be starting up soon."

He grabbed her arm. "Are you sure you're okay?"

"For now I have to be." And she believed that. "What are the other lawyers going to think when Candice doesn't return? Are they all in on it?"

"I don't know. It would be pretty crazy to have that many players in the know."

"Walk with me." She started walking back toward the courtroom. "This was the first time I'd ever met her or heard of her. The other two guys are the regular counsel."

"Then that would make sense that she was sent in just for this job. I'm not saying the Cyber Future lawyers are clean. But they might have a limited role in what is happening to you."

"Where have you been hiding?" Sam tugged on her arm. "We're about to start again. I think the judge is going to let them do their opening statement, then we'll break for lunch and have ours."

"Your opening is solid, Sam. I feel good about it."

"Thanks." He turned to look at Gabe. "Is everything all right?"

"Yes. Focus on your work for now, and I'll make sure things run smoothly."

She was grateful that Gabe didn't get into what had happened with Candice right now. Sam needed to be thinking about the lawsuit. Regardless of her woes, the case was happening.

Hope took her seat next to Sam and gave Lee a quick smile. No one on the outside would know that she had just been held at gunpoint. She'd always been good at compartmentalizing. Mostly because of her childhood. But she was amazed that she was able to really keep it together. A lot of that had to do with knowing that Gabe really did have her back. She quietly thanked God for sending Gabe into her life. And for him stopping Candice.

She'd been distant from her faith—a faith that was fledgling to begin with. But over the past week she'd started to feel drawn to God again. Even when she wanted to pull back and blame Him for the awful events of her past and the scary threats to her now, she heard a voice that told her just the opposite. To trust in Him. She was still alive, and that had to be for a reason.

Settling into her chair, she opened her laptop ready to take notes of Walter's opening statement. After the judge gave his standard admonishments, Walter took to the podium. She was interested to see what tactic he would take. How would he attempt to relate to the small town southern jury?

"Ladies and gentleman," he said. "My name is Walter Herring. I represent Cyber Future in this case. And we are the plaintiffs in this action. We are the ones who are bringing suit against Wakefield Corporation for breach of contract."

He walked out from behind the podium, seemingly at ease and strode closer to the jury box. "I'm not going to pretend to be an insider. Everyone knows that I'm from a big law firm in California. And that we represent Cyber Future, a large corporation based in California." He paused and looked at the jury. "But I also know this. You've been given instructions by the judge, and you're going to follow those even if you dislike Cyber Future or me for that matter. You can dislike me all you want, but you aren't allowed under the law to hold that against my client. And you may dislike my client too, but once again you aren't allowed to hold that against them."

Sam shot up out of his chair. "Objection, your honor. I let this go on for a minute, but I think Mr. Herring's speech is veering off a bit into prohibited argument." Hope wasn't surprised that Sam made the objection. Opening statement was all about what the evidence was going to show. Lawyers weren't allowed to do what Walter was trying to accomplish by making arguments. That would only be proper for closing arguments.

"I tend to agree, Mr. Upton. Mr. Herring, I think you've established your point for the jury. Please proceed with your opening statement focusing on what the evidence will show."

"Of course, Your Honor. Thank you." He walked a couple of steps backward and then stopped. "Ladies and gentleman of the jury. What the evidence will show in this case is that Cyber Future entered into a distribution contract with Wakefield Corporation for the sale of the Wakefield Chip. While Cyber Future diligently held up its end of the bargain, the evidence will show that Wakefield breached the contract by failing to pay Cyber Future the amount it was due under the contract."

For the next half an hour, Hope took copious notes as Walter presented his opening statement. He was relaxed, persuasive, and intelligent. Hope would feel a lot better if she didn't have the knowledge she did about Nola. And the fact that Wakefield was in breach.

Hope also studied the jury. Trying desperately to get a read. The jury was made up of seven women and five men plus one female alternate. They were paying attention and many of them were taking notes. She had no doubt that many of them were pro

Wakefield, but she also thought that they would take their civic duty and the instructions provided by the judge seriously.

"All right, ladies and gentleman of the jury," Judge Masters said. "We're going to take an hour lunch break. Then we will reconvene and hear opening statement from the defense. I will remind you at each break that you are not to discuss the case amongst yourself nor talk about the case to anyone else or on any social media." He sighed. "I remember the good ole' days when we didn't have the internet, and these things didn't need to be said over and over again. But I have zero tolerance for any of that in my courtroom. Everyone understand?"

A murmur of noise came from the jury.

"All rise," the bailiff said loudly.

Hope stood up and had Walter's opening running through her mind. All in all he hadn't said anything she wasn't expecting. Unfortunately for them, he'd been more persuasive than she had anticipated. Sam didn't seem fazed though.

"For lunch breaks we're just going to be walking back to Greg's firm and having lunch brought in from local places each day," Sam said. "I'm interested to hear if you think I need to make any adjustments based on Walter's opening."

They started walking out of the courtroom followed by the rest of their contingent. Hope felt an elevated sense of importance. Sam was looking to her for advice and insight. All of the work was paying off.

She glanced over her shoulder and Gabe scowled. He wasn't comfortable with this situation. That much was painfully obvious to her.

* * *

Sitting in the law firm that night around the conference room table, Gabe knew what he had to do. And he also knew that doing it was critical to keeping Hope safe, but could be the end to building a relationship. Today had been too much of a close call.

It bothered him that he'd had side conversations with Caleb, Lee, and lastly Sam. But they'd all agreed it was the right thing to do. And of course they all thought he was the perfect person to break the news. They promised they'd back him up. So they sat around the conference room table having just finished up their dinner.

It was now or never. Sam started the discussion. "Hope, there's something we need to discuss."

She looked at him, her eyes lit up with anticipation. "Okay. I don't know about you, but I'm excited about tomorrow. Your opening was the perfect counterpoint to Walter's. You really pulled them back into our court. And I think we can do some damage on cross examination of their witnesses. And…"

Sam held up his hand. "Gabe, why don't you tell Hope what we all discussed."

Uh oh. Sam wasn't doing a good job of setting this up. Hope narrowed her eyes at him.

Before he could say anything, she leaned forward in her seat. "So, you guys have been talking about me?" The accusation rolled off her tongue.

"It's not like that, Hope. That's why Caleb joined us after dinner. He wanted to be here for this discussion. He and I let everyone know what happened at the courthouse today. And after further questioning of Candice and an examination of all the facts we know, we think the only way to keep you safe is for you to leave Maxwell."

"No way." She stood up from her chair. "I can't believe you all making decisions about me as if I have no say so." She turned to Sam. "You're the only one who can make me leave. You know how hard I've worked on this case. You also know that you really need me to try this. It would be difficult without me."

Sam looked down and then back up at Hope. "Hope, if there was any other way, I would be all for it. You're so right. You deserve this chance. You've more than earned this opportunity. But you're also one of the lawyers in my firm. I'm responsible for you while you're here. And no job, even if it's your dream job and your dream trial, is worth risking your life."

"But, Sam."

"Let me finish," he said. He stood up from his chair and walked over to face her. "There will be other opportunities, Hope. When you have talent, real talent like what you have, there will be other ways for you to gain experiences and demonstrate what you can do. The only way you'll have a future at the firm is if you're safe. And after what happened today, I'm convinced you aren't safe here."

She turned away from Sam and walked toward Gabe. "You're the one who agreed with me that they'll just follow me wherever I go."

"Which is even more reason to get you to a truly safe location until we can locate and neutralize the threat," he said.

"And if I refuse."

"I'm sorry, Hope," Sam said. "This is non-negotiable. You'll leave Maxwell with Gabe. You will not be in court tomorrow."

He watched as she turned a bit pale. But she didn't say a word. She grabbed her laptop and her purse and walked out of the room.

"I knew that was going to happen," Gabe said.

"She'll see in the long term that it was the only option," Sam said.

"I've got to go after her," he said. Then he jogged out of the room. She couldn't have gotten far. But to say that she would be angry at him would be the understatement of his career. He needed to deal with the issue head on. Take the beating and try to move on.

"Hope," he called.

She didn't turn around. He caught up to her and grabbed her arm.

"Don't you dare touch me." Her eyes were ablaze. "You were supposed to have my back, remember? And I was stupid enough to believe that you could be different. That you really did have my back."

"Hope, I do. I'm doing this because I care so much about you. Even at the risk of knowing what this could do to us. I can't have you put in this type of danger anymore. I just can't do it."

"Let's be clear, Gabe. There is no us. I may not be able to get away from you right now, but when I do, I don't want you in my life. And I surely pray that I never come back to this awful town again."

He let her say those things because she was upset. And rightfully so. Maybe with time she'd forgive him, but he wasn't so sure. "We'll go by the hotel and get all of your things. Then stop by my place. Zeke's going to stay with Caleb while we're gone."

"And you don't even know how long that will be." Her voice was louder than he'd ever heard it.

"No, Hope. I don't. As long as it takes to keep you safe."

By the time they'd reached his place, she'd only said a few words to him. Mainly about moving her stuff. He would need patience and understanding to get through this.

They walked into this house, and she grabbed onto his arm. "You said something that is really bothering me."

"What's that?"

"As long as it takes." She paused. "Are you thinking about putting me into witness protection?"

Her grip was tight on his arm. "My boss did bring that up."

"And?"

"Everything is on the table right now. But we also agreed that it would be a bit premature to think about the Witness Security Program at this point."

"But it hasn't been ruled out?" She let go of his arm and looked up.

He couldn't help it. He had to try to comfort her. He pulled her into his arms. "Hope, I'm sorry. I don't want it to come to that. I'm going to do everything I can to make sure it doesn't, but I'm not going to lie to you. No secrets. It's a possibility."

She pulled back from his embrace and looked in his eyes. "That would destroy everything I've worked for. Do you understand that?"

"You can't think of it like that. You have to think of it as a fresh start."

She broke away from him and started pacing back and forth in the living room.

"What would I do? I know I couldn't be a lawyer since that's what I do now. Everything, Gabe. Everything! I told you how I grew up. Poor with an awful family life. No stability. I worked my way through school and have done everything and more to excel at the firm. To have that ripped away from me is unfathomable."

He walked over to her and lifted her chin up. "Hope, listen to yourself. What's the theme? You're a fighter. Whatever challenge is put in front of you, you take it head on. Without fear, and with full determination. It's one of the things I admire the most about you."

"Admire?"

"Yes, admire. I know we haven't known each other but for a short time. In that time, though, I've seen you face down threats and get back up. Never once did it occur to you to cut and run. Because you're not a cut and run type of woman. And if we could stay and fight we would. But this is one time where we have to hunker down."

"Even if it means me losing everything?"

"I think even as you're saying these things, you realize that your career isn't everything. Being with you has taught me that about my own career. I know you think that we come from different worlds, but we're more alike that you believe. I've put my work ahead of everything else. And I had this bull headed idea that I could find someone to neatly fit into my world and live happily ever after."

"What do you mean?" she asked quietly.

"What I mean is that you've changed all of that, Hope. My career is still very important to me. But I want more out of life than just being an FBI agent at the top of my game. I want someone special to share life with. To laugh and to talk and to bear the burdens together. I've been so caught up in my plans and goals that I've gotten myself to believe in something that doesn't exist. I believe the Lord brought you into my life to show me another path."

"I honestly don't know what to say."

"You don't have to say anything. I know we're in a crazy situation and things have been moving quickly. But know that I don't want to let you go, Hope. I refuse to. And if that means going into witness protection with you, I would."

"You would give up your career in the FBI for me?"

"Without hesitation."

She grabbed his hands and tears welled up in her eyes. "No one has ever been willing to sacrifice for me. Ever."

"You're stuck with me now. We're a team, and we're going to get through this together. I know you're angry at the situation, but I really hope you won't stay angry at me." He brought her hand up to his mouth and kissed it.

"You tell me what we need to do. And I'll do it."

He smiled. Her fight was back. This was the Hope he needed right now. "I'm going to pack my bag. Then we are going to hit the road."

"To where? It's already getting late."

"I'll be fine driving. I want to put some distance between us and Maxwell. They won't be expecting you to be leaving during the trial. So we need to get as far away as possible as quickly as we can."

"Why not fly?"

"We'd be easier to track that way."

"What about FBI transport?" she asked.

He smiled. "Come with me while I pack, and I'll fill you in."

She walked up the steps to his room and he pulled out a suitcase and a duffel. "Since I told you no secrets, there's one more thing you should know."

"All right. What is it?"

"My boss and I think there may be a mole in the Bureau."

"A mole at the FBI?" she asked.

"Yeah. I know it sounds crazy, but this type of thing does happen. Especially when you're dealing with organized crime. The agent could be being blackmailed or be motivated by money."

She looked out the window in his room into the darkness of the night. "What made you suspect a mole?"

"I think someone has been accessing my reports on the investigation that I've been putting in the system and sending to my boss. I have the tech guys looking into it, but for now, we need to be extra careful."

"The bad guys are everywhere," she said softly.

"But don't worry. I've got a plan to flush out the mole. We're going to feed false intel through the system on our location and what our plans are for protecting you."

"That's smart. I assume you can trust your boss?"

"Hope, if I can't trust my boss, then I'm in a world of hurt."

She walked over to him as he threw socks in the duffel bag. "That wasn't a yes."

"It was a yes. I do trust him, but beyond him, I can't say for sure. I'm definitely not willing to risk your life over it." He grabbed a few more things and put them in the duffle. "Grab us nonperishables from the kitchen while I finish up here. I'll only be a minute."

She nodded. "Thank you, Gabe. I know I lashed out earlier, but I do appreciate what you're doing here."

Before he could respond, she walked out of the room.

Lord, please help me keep her safe. You've brought her into my life. I can't lose her now.

He grabbed his bag and a shot rang out piercing the silence in the room.

CHAPTER ELEVEN

Hope hit the ground when she heard the first shot. Thankfully, she wasn't hit, but she was staying low. Crouched down behind the island in the kitchen.

"Hope," Gabe's voice rang out.

"I'm okay," she yelled.

But then more shots were fired. It sounded louder than fireworks on the fourth of July. By speaking she'd given away her location. A bullet pierced through the wood cabinet above her head.

"Run, Hope," Gabe yelled.

But there was no way she was running. She heard loud noises and grunts. Peering out from behind the island she saw that Gabe was fighting the gunman. She should use this chance to get away, but Gabe was in danger. Two against one was always better odds even if she didn't really have any fighting skill. What she did have was her brain and the element of surprise.

The gunman was gaining the upper hand, but he was facing away from her. She looked around the kitchen for something heavy she could use. Quickly, she grabbed the crock pot and scurried into the living room where the men were fighting.

Saying a quick prayer, she made her move. The gunman was so focused on Gabe, he had no idea she had come up right behind him. With all the strength she could muster, she swung the crock pot using two hands and slammed it into the gunman's head. He dropped to the floor with a thud.

"Hope! You could've gotten killed," Gabe said. "I told you to run."

"We're a team remember?" She paused, looking down at the man. "Is he alive?"

Gabe crouched down and checked for a pulse. "Yes. I'll cuff him and have the police come and pick him up. But it doesn't change the plan. We've got to get out of here." Gabe grabbed the man and threw him over his shoulder. "Get the keys from the counter. Go to the car, lock the doors. I'll be right out."

Hope nodded and took the keys from the kitchen counter. She'd almost killed a man. But thankfully she hadn't. She'd done what was necessary to protect Gabe and herself.

Sitting in the car in the dark, she took a few deep breaths steadying herself. Could she really expect to feel calm right now?

A knock on the window broke her out of those thoughts with a start. It was Gabe. She unlocked the door, and he threw a bag in the backseat. Then he slid behind the wheel.

"So much for them waiting," she said.

"Yeah, but it doesn't mean anything. They still may assume that you'll be back in court. But they wanted to get to you since Candice didn't get the job done."

"And we're back to the nebulous *they*."

"The crime syndicate connected to Cyber Future. At this point, that's the best description I can give it."

"And we still don't know why. Why would they be willing to go to such great lengths to capture or kill me for?" She asked more to herself.

"I'm glad you brought that up again. My boss has been working with an outside security consultant that the FBI uses. He specializes in organized crime. He's been digging into the groups in California trying to see if there's been word on the streets there about any trouble brewing. That way it's outside the FBI, but we can still get the information. Hopefully, we'll hear back from him soon."

"That was very smart."

"But figuring that out isn't my top priority. Keeping you safe is."

"Where are we headed?"

"How do you feel about the beach?"

She smiled. "You know, believe it or not. I've only been to the beach once. And I loved it." She paused. "It's actually one of the only good memories I have of my entire childhood. I don't know how we afforded it. Dad probably won a bet or something. He was as addicted to gambling as mom was to the alcohol. But we rented a car and drove to the beach for a week one summer when I was in elementary school. I remember thinking that I wanted those moments to last forever. If only I could just live there, then everything would be better."

"But it never got any better."

"Far from it. Although that week was the highlight of my childhood. Mom drank as usual, but she didn't get violently drunk. We played out by the ocean, built sandcastles, and I dipped my feet in the water because I couldn't swim. Still can't swim." Her mind trailed back to those days. Her heart ached for those moments that she would never experience again.

"Sounds like it was a fun week."

"It was. But then once we got back home, the fights between my parents started again. Some were violent. I hid in my room. Trying to pretend like I was still at the beach, that I could hear the ocean waves and feel the sand beneath my feet. I brought back a seashell, and I'd hold onto it for comfort. I know that seems silly and childish, but it provided me with a small measure of peace. I just wanted to block out the world and be taken back to the sunny beach. To feel the warm breeze tickle my nose. And just for a moment to pretend that I was a normal little girl with a family that loved her."

He reached over and grabbed her hand. "I'm so sorry that your childhood was so difficult. But you've come through it, Hope. Like I said, you're a fighter. And just like you made it through those difficult times, you're going to make it through these too."

"I know," she said softly. "But when times get trying, those old wounds open."

"You have your faith now though, Hope. Something you didn't have then."

"I know. And getting to know you and even this entire experience has made me want to seek out God again. There's simply no other explanation for why I'm still alive, other than to say that it was God's will. And I'm at peace with that."

"Hope, we're all at the mercy of God's will."

"I know that now."

"Try to get some rest. I'll be fine driving."

"That doesn't seem fair."

"No reason for us both to be awake all night. And I promise if I get too tired, I'll wake you up."

"Promise?"

"Yes."

***

Gabe heard her soft breathing as he kept his eyes on the road. He was so amped up. There was no way he could sleep even if he weren't driving. Running on pure adrenaline and desire to keep the woman he loved safe, he kept driving.

Love. That's really what it was. There was no running from it. He loved Hope Finch. And while he was perfectly comfortable with those feelings, he had a sneaking suspicion that she would not be. At least not yet. For now he would keep those thoughts to himself.

He looked over at her sleeping peacefully and felt a strong surge of protection running through his body. He would not let anything happen to this woman. The only woman he had ever really loved in any romantic way.

Her exhaustion was evident by the fact that the sun was beginning to rise and she still slept. The good news was that they were in Florida. About to roll into the beach town of Summer Breeze. It was a touristy mid-sized city that would fit their needs perfectly. Not a big city, but not so small as to be noticed.

He pulled into a large beachfront hotel where he'd already reserved two adjoining rooms on the drive down. He hated to wake her but it was time.

Gently he nudged her shoulder. "Hope, we're here."

She mumbled something and then awoke with eyes wide.

"It's okay, Hope. It's Gabe. We're in Florida. At a hotel right on the beach."

"Wow. That seemed like no time at all."

He laughed. "About six hours."

"I slept like a log." She looked out the window. "So this is it."

"Welcome to Summer Breeze, Florida."

He opened the car door and was met by a nice breeze and the sound of crashing waves. He watched as she exited the car and stood facing the ocean. Her long blonde hair had fallen out of its bun and blew in the wind.

"A lot different than Maxwell," she said.

"And no one knows we're here. Literally just you and me. At least for the time being."

"Not even your boss?"

"Not yet. I'll decide when and if it makes sense. For now we decided it best to have complete secrecy. We're going to feed false information about our whereabouts into the system though. Then we'll have an FBI team follow up to see if we can smoke out the mole." He paused and looked at her. "Stay in the lobby where I can see you. But I'm going to get our rooms. And I also brought you a hat to wear."

"Great," she said, eyeing the cap warily. "Next you'll want me to become a redhead and chop my hair off. No wait, we'll save that for when you put me into witness protection."

He pulled her close. "Don't talk like that, okay. Let's stay positive. Take a deep breath. Smell the ocean. We're going to be fine."

She smiled. "All right."

"Let me get the rooms."

By the time they were settled in, it was midmorning and he was ready for a big breakfast or a nap. Or both. He grabbed Hope from her room and walked down the beach. He'd gotten a great recommendation for a breakfast spot right on the ocean.

"You need to eat and then sleep," she said. "You won't be good to anyone if you're sleep deprived."

"I'll take a nap after we eat."

"That brings up a good point, you know. What are we supposed to do with our time? It's not like I can do any legal work right now considering my main case is in trial. What will I do?'

"Let's just take it one day at a time. For today, just try to get some rest and get adjusted. Tomorrow will be another day and probably another challenge."

She nodded, seemingly accepting his point.

"This is it, Breezy Beach Restaurant."

"Oh, this is cute," she said.

They stood in front of the restaurant that had a huge wrap around porch.

"Don't worry. I'll ask that we sit outside."

"Do you think that's safe?"

"For now, yes. I was very careful on the way down. There was no one following, and I haven't seen anything out of the ordinary."

"But still."

"Remember, Hope. Absolutely no one knows that we're here. I used a cover identity to check into our rooms. One that's never been used before. There is no tracing us to this hotel. It's just you and me right now."

She smiled. "That isn't so bad, is it?"

"It's not bad at all." He grabbed her hand and they walked up the steps to Breezy Beach Restaurant. The best breakfast on the beach, or so he'd been told.

"A table for two, outside please," he told he hostess.

"Right this way." The smiling young woman led them to a table on the porch at the corner. It couldn't have been more perfect. He could see his future with Hope clear as day. A future different than what he thought he wanted, but now everything he knew he was truly looking for.

They ordered and then looked at each other, neither one of them saying a word.

"What are you thinking?" she asked.

"Too much."

"Me too." She paused. "It's just so strange. Not too long ago I was sitting in my office at Rice and Taylor doing my work, and now I'm here. On the run. Fearing for my life. And then there's you."

"I hope I'm not a negative in all of this."

"One of the only positives." She reached out and touched his hand. "I know I've been a bit difficult at times. But I wanted to thank you for everything you've done. We haven't always agreed on the same strategy but in the end, I understand that you've had my best interest in mind."

They finished eating and Hope smiled at him. "How about a walk down the beach?"

"Sounds perfect."

They exited the restaurant and walked down the soft sand until they got closer to the water.

"This does bring back a lot of memories." She stared out at the ocean.

His phone rang, and he looked at the screen. "It's the consultant that my boss hired. I need to take this."

"Marino," he answered.

"This is Steve. I've got some answers for you."

"Give it to me."

"I'm not sure you're going to want to hear it."

"Let me put you on speaker so Hope can hear this too."

"Okay."

He pushed the speaker button. "We're here, Steve."

"Thanks. So I started working my sources and here's what I've been able to find out." He paused. "This chip everyone is talking about actually contains a list."

"What kind of list?" Hope asked.

"That's the sticking point. I don't have exact rock solid intel on that, but I have enough. That list contains the names of corporate executives with ties to organized crime. So Cyber Future execs are on it, but there are others on it as well. It was supposed to be used almost as a rolodex for corporate America contacts that can be used to further illegal enterprise. This list is not only highly valuable but considered top secret given how that knowledge would impact those executives if it was ever made known."

"Because whoever has it," Gabe said, "would hold a lot of power. Think about all the blackmail opportunity there."

"Yeah, no doubt," Steve said. "So it appears that Nola, being the enterprising man he is, was able to steal the chip. He probably recognized the value and what he could do to advance his own businesses. And this is where it gets bad for Hope. The prevailing knowledge on the street was that Hope was helping facilitate all of this through her law firm. People believe that Hope not only has seen the list, but is actually serving as the keeper of the list, too. No one believes Nola has it. They all think it's Hope."

"Wow," she said.

"Yeah, so the endgame was to capture you, find out where the list is, destroy it and then…"

"Then kill me," she said.

Silence.

"Is Nola the one responsible for making Hope a target?" Gabe asked.

"I don't know. It could be that the Cyber Future cronies saw them together and make the jump themselves. Or Nola could've fed them the false information trying to divert attention away from himself."

"But the bottom line is that I'm still not safe. As long as they think I have access to the list, they'll be coming after me."

"Sorry I don't have better news," Steve said. "I'm going to keep working and see if I can come up with anything else that could be helpful. I'll check in later."

The call ended and he stood there looking at Hope. "What are you thinking?"

She turned to face him, her brown eyes wide. "How could this have happened to me? Is God punishing me?"

He pulled her to him and hugged her close. Then after a moment he stepped back. "God is not punishing you, Hope. Don't even think like that."

"But for those two years I spent with Barry. And Barry was so openly hostile to faith, and I didn't do anything. I didn't speak up."

"God is good, Hope. He's also forgiving and understanding. It doesn't matter about your past. All that matters is where you're at now. And now that we know what the issues are, we are better able to address it."

"What, by hiding me away?"

"At this exact moment, yes. But if I have anything to do with it, not forever."

"Gabe, I'm tired of running. I want to go back."

"That's just not going to happen."

"Face it head on. End this."

"How so?"

"Taking it head on. Going back into that courtroom."

"Even if we were to use you as bait, which is what I think you're suggesting, catching a random hit man or woman isn't going to solve your problem. We need to get to the source."

"What better source than the Cyber Future execs who are currently sitting in that courtroom?"

"Hope, these people may be corporate executives, but they're also criminals. You can't just stroll in there and reason with them."

"Why not? Why can't I tell them I don't know anything?"

"And you and I both know they won't believe a word of that."

"Why can't I try?"

"It's too dangerous."

She nodded. "I think I'd like to go take a nap."

"Sure. This is stressful. I could use a little rest myself." He had to come up with a plan, before it was too late.

CHAPTER TWELVE

Hope realized that Gabe would be furious with her, but she had no choice. She knew what she had to do. She couldn't stay here hidden on this beach waiting for them to find her.

She grabbed her small bag and looked around outside the hotel room. Not seeing anyone, she made her way down to the lobby. She caught a plane back to Atlanta, and then arrived back in Maxwell in time for the afternoon session at court.

When she walked into the courtroom and sat at counsel's table, Sam's eyes widened.

"What in the world are you doing here?"

"Handling things my way, sir."

Sam couldn't exactly make a scene, so he nodded and prepared for his cross examination of the next Cyber Future witness.

Hope eyed the other side of the courtroom cautiously. Just as she'd expected, the key Cyber Future executives were sitting there right behind the counsel table. At the three thirty p.m. break, she followed them out of the courtroom.

"Excuse me," she said.

The taller of the two men, turned around. "Yes?"

"I think you know who I am."

"I'm sorry, ma'am. Do we know you?"

"Don't play stupid with me. I know about the list, I know about you, I know about everything."

The man who spoke narrowed his dark eyes at her. "Why don't we take this conversation outside?"

"What so you can call in one of your shooters to try to take me out? Again? No. I've had enough. You either talk now or I publish the list live on every news and social media outlet there is."

"You wouldn't dare." The other man said.

"I would."

The taller man grabbed her arm.

"Let go of her," Gabe's voice commanded.

She was really in trouble now. She didn't know if she was more afraid of Gabe's reaction or the Cyber Future execs. But listening to Gabe, the man dropped her arm.

"You don't know who you're dealing with," he said, first looking at Gabe and then back to Hope.

"I think I have a pretty clear idea. So this is how it's going to go. You're going to stop your attempts on my life. If something happens to me I have it set up so the list goes live. It's that simple." She saw the flash of surprise go through Gabe's eyes.

"Why would we negotiate with you? You could always hold that list over our heads."

"That's your problem not mine. And just because I'm a practical girl, I've made arrangements. If anything happens to me. And I mean anything, that list will be made public immediately."

The man sucked in a breath. Would he believe her?

"We'll consider your offer." The two skulked away.

Now she had to deal with her even bigger problem. Gabe.

"Did you really think you could sneak away without me knowing?" he asked. He guided her down the hallway. "What about us being a team?"

"I knew you'd never go for my idea. Even if it was a solid one."

"And what have you really accomplished besides making them mad?"

"I think I've accomplished a whole lot."

"Yeah, except the part when they challenge you and you don't have the list. Or they decide to take their chances and kill you anyway because you're too much of a threat."

She couldn't help but laugh. "Are you forgetting that they've already tried multiple times? This has to stop, and it's the best way."

"No. I'm getting you out of here, now."

She stood, hands on her hip. "You can't make me. What are you going to drag me out of the courthouse?"

"If I have to, yes, I will. It's too dangerous, Hope. Let's go."

"I'll leave now, but I'm not leaving Maxwell. Understood?"

He frowned but then nodded.

***

Hope didn't have much to say to him. She'd insisted that she would be back in court tomorrow. There was nothing he could do but go with her and try to keep her safe.

Sam had given up his quest of keeping her away, but basically told her, no, it was her decision.

Driving up to the courthouse, he had to say something. "This roller coaster we've been on will end at some point. And I still hope that we can talk about moving forward together."

"I've been doing a lot of thinking about that. And I just don't see how we could make it work. I live in New York. Your life is here."

"I can move."

"You'll what?" she said softly.

"Yes, I will move."

"I thought you said you wanted to stay here. Get married, have kids, all that. Here in Maxwell."

"I did. But if the choice is between losing you and leaving here, I'll move."

"Wouldn't you be resentful?"

"I always thought I would be. But that was before you. You changed it all for me, Hope."

She didn't respond and threads of fear pulsed through him. Had he moved too fast? Been too open about his ever growing feelings?

"Let's get through this, Gabe. Then we can figure all of that out."

He'd have to take that for now. She didn't tell him no way.

Parking his new rental in the town square, it was time for another day in court.

"I need to go to the conference room for a meeting before court starts today."

"I'll go with you."

"All right."

"Which conference room?"

"Sam's message said room B."

They walked down the long corridor into Room B.

"Looks like we beat him here. He wanted to talk over the cross examination of the next Cyber Future witness."

They sat at the table and she pulled out her laptop and started clicking. After a few minutes, a loud noise started blaring.

"That's the emergency alarm. We need to get out of here," he said.

"Are you sure that's what it is?"

"Yeah. I've been here during the drills before."

He went to the door and pulled but it didn't budge. "The door won't open." His pulse raced. The door was heavy and fortified from the courtroom renovations. Room B had been the designated room in case of emergencies and the door was made of extra strong metal materials. He felt like such an idiot. They'd totally been played.

"Oh no," she said.

"This is a trap." Just as he said it, his phone started to ring.

"Yes," he answered.

"I assume Hope is there with you," the male voice said.

"Who is this?"

"Just making sure you two were where you were supposed to be. Listen to me. Have Hope turn over the file, or I will detonate the device that is currently under the conference room table."

"A bomb?" he asked.

Hope's mouth dropped open at his words.

"Yes. You have ten minutes. They start now."

He didn't have a second to waste. "Listen to me, Hope. I need you to help me. Use this flashlight app on the phone and shine it up on the table." He crawled up under the table to see what they were dealing with. He was thankful for those extra classes he'd taken with the bomb squad, but he was far from an expert. He let out a sigh of relief and prayer of thanks when he saw the device taped up under the table.

"What are you going to do?" she asked.

"I feel like I have a better than fifty percent chance of disarming this thing. But if I mess up, it will detonate." He pulled his small pocket knife out of his jacket.

"I have faith in you, Gabe. What is our timeframe?"

"They said you have ten minutes to turn over the list or they blow us up."

"Then you better get started."

"I could use a prayer right now."

"Even if I turn over the list, they're still going to try to kill us, aren't they?"

"Yes," he said quietly. "But keep that light shining on this device, and I believe I can do this. I also need you to let me know my time." He looked at the blinking timer on the bomb. "I need a five minute countdown, because we've already used time. I don't want to focus on the timer, I need you to do that for me."

Gabe prayed as he worked. Taking extra care to focus on cutting the right wires.

"Two minutes left," she said.

He only had one more wire left to cut. This was it. He had to choose the correct wire. If this was the wrong choice, they were going to die. *Please, Lord. I need your guidance now.* He took a breath and cut the wire. The timer beeped and stopped at one minute thirty-two seconds.

"It's done," he said.

She pulled him up from under the table and hugged him. "Thank you, Gabe. Once again for saving my life."

"It's not over yet, Hope. Once they figure out that we disabled the bomb, they'll try something else. We're still locked in here. There wasn't any time to call Caleb before, but now I will. He'll have to help us get out of here."

Just then a loud boom rocked the building, and he hit the floor hard busting open his lip. He tasted blood.

"Another bomb," he said. "Stay down, Hope." He crawled over to the door and pushed again. The bomb must have loosened it because it came open.

He ran over to Hope and grabbed her off the ground. "Let's move."

Smoke billowed through the hallway filling his lungs. Then a rapid succession of shots rang out. He dove toward Hope, covering her with his body. And then he felt the burning pain in his shoulder, before the world went black.

***

Blood poured onto Hope, and she heard herself scream. Gabe had been shot. She had to get him out of there. Flames started to move closer to them. Gabe's body was heavy, but she willed herself to drag him down the hall. She grabbed up under his arms and tugged him making slow progress. *Lord, I need your strength right now. Please help me save this man.*

She kept going and then she heard a man's voice ring out. "Hope, Gabe!"

It was Caleb.

"Over here," she yelled as she choked on the smoke.

A minute later, Caleb was standing over her. "He's been shot. Can you carry him? I can walk on my own."

When they approached the side exit, she waited until Caleb was out with Gabe before she followed. The only person she truly felt like she could trust right now beside Gabe was Caleb.

Had Sam really been the one to lure her there to that room? Or had his email been hacked?

A medic was working on Gabe. Caleb turned to her. "He's going to be fine. It looks like a lot of blood, but the bullet went straight through. I've seen plenty of wounds like that during my tours."

Yes, she remembered that he was in the military. "I don't know if we can trust anyone."

"I've got the two Cyber Future executives in holding."

"Sam is the one who sent me the message to get us to that conference room. Or someone using his email."

"I haven't seen Sam today."

Her stomach dropped. "He has to be in on it then."

"I'm sorry, Hope."

"What about Nola?"

"He's with Lee. They're not technically being detained but they're not going anywhere until we figure this out. I'll put a BOLO out for Sam."

She walked over to Gabe lying on a gurney, an EMT close by. She grabbed his hand. "Gabe, I know Caleb said you were going to be fine, but I need you to be okay?"

"Ma'am, I'm sorry. We're about to transport him to the hospital."

She nodded.

Caleb put his hand on her shoulder. "I'm going to need you to stick with me. For your own safety. We'll head to the station and try to sort this all out."

***

Gabe woke up with a pounding pain in his arm and a hazy memory of what had happened. "Hope." It came out as only a whisper. His throat burning with dryness.

"I'm right here, Gabe."

Thank, God. He opened his eyes and saw her. Her hair hanging down, her eyes filled with tears.

"How long have I been out?"

"Overnight. They gave you some meds for the pain so that probably had something to do with it."

"And what about everyone else?"

"The Cyber Future executives are in FBI custody. Nola and Lee are being questioned. And Sam is still MIA." She paused. "I just can't believe that he was involved in this. It was like he had it planned all along."

"You think he did?"

"Yes. It all makes sense now, in a twisted way. Having me be the one to step into the trial because of my connection with Nola. I think this has been a Sam operation from the beginning. He was working with and against the Cyber Future guys. Nola just happened to be part of the game. But not the one behind the attacks on me."

He closed his eyes trying to process this all. "So what's Sam's angle in all of this?"

"Well, that remains to be seen. I think he might have used me as the fall girl, and he's the one who has the list. So he was double crossing the Cyber Future guys. The bigger issue is whether Nola and Sam are working together and if Lee knows."

"That's pretty ingenious. Make the competition think that you're working with them, and have them do the dirty work. In the end you are gone, he has the list to do whatever he wants with, and he's perfectly in the clear. All suspicions are either on you or Nola."

"Yeah, and right now, no one knows where he is. He could be in another country by now. He has the money from his years of being a partner, the connections, everything."

A knock sounded at the door. Gabe looked over and weakly smiled. "Ben."

"How're you doing?"

"I've been better, but told it could've been much worse." He paused and looked over at her. "Hope Finch this is my boss at the FBI I've told you about, Ben Cook."

"Nice to meet you." She outstretched her hand. "Although I wish it were under better circumstances."

"Me too, Ms. Finch."

"Please call me Hope."

He nodded. "I wanted to give you an update. We're on the manhunt for Sam Upton. I also have Steve working the case too. We will find him."

"And how far does this thing spread?" he asked.

"The Cyber Future guys have lawyered up, but they are clearly looking to cut a deal. So we'll see how the district attorney wants to play it. But I'd be in favor of making a deal if we can get to the bottom of this."

"And whether Nola and Lee are involved," Hope said quietly.

"There's no doubt Nola is up to something, but the evidence tying him to this particular crime plot is more at the accessory level. He probably stole that chip without knowing what was on it. Before he could determine the contents, it was stolen by Sam."

"That's consistent with what Nola told me," Hope said. "Sam used him."

"Yes. It was a convenient cover for his subterfuge. He probably knows that Nola's hands are already dirty, so it was the combination of having Nola and you, Hope, that let him do his work."

"Sam gets the list, and I get killed."

"Basically he thought he'd created the perfect crime. But there's no such thing," Gabe said.

"And we don't know what Sam was planning to do with the list. But he must've been responsible for taking it from the file room once Nola gave it to me."

"Has he gotten a lawyer too?" Gabe asked.

"Of course. But Lee is encouraging him to cooperate," Ben said.

Gabe closed his eyes.

"We should let him get some rest," Hope said.

"Yes," Ben said. "I'll check back in later."

"You should sleep," she said.

"All right. But don't go anywhere."

"Don't worry. You're not getting rid of me that easy."

***

A week later, Hope was throwing the ball to Zeke in Gabe's back yard. Gabe was bouncing back quickly, but ball throwing was against doctor's orders.

"Hope," Gabe yelled from the porch. "Mom just dropped off some lunch if you're hungry."

"Maybe in a little bit." She looked at Zeke practically smiling with the tennis ball in his mouth. "All right, Zekester. I need a little rest."

She walked up to the porch and took a seat beside Gabe. The weather was in the fifties. And Hope loved the feeling of the fresh air.

"I thought you two might be out here." Caleb walked around the back yard and through the fence. Ben was with him.

"We've got news," Ben said. "And we wanted to deliver it in person."

Zeke ran to greet his favorite pet sitter Caleb.

"Have a seat." Gabe motioned to the chairs on the porch.

"We got him," Ben said. "Sam Upton is in FBI custody. Tracked down at the Canadian border."

Her heart thumped wildly. "Really?" Was this nightmare actually over?

"Yes. It's him, and he's begging for a deal. So we should know everything soon."

"What about the ties to organized crime in California?" Hope asked.

"Now that the FBI has the list, we're launching a full-fledged investigation to every executive on that list. The ties to organized crime run deep, but since the individuals have been put on alert, there's no risk to you any more, Hope. It will also be on the news soon that Sam Upton is the criminal behind this massive list. It's one of the biggest white collar and organized crime investigation that the FBI has ever seen. It will probably be ongoing for years."

"Wow," she said.

"Nola is being held on accessory and theft charges, but we'll have to see if it sticks. We're also examining fraud charges based on what you were able to tell us, Hope, about the lawsuit with Cyber Future on the breach of contract. And the Cyber Future guys are taking a deal that the district attorney cut."

"Thank you for everything you've both done," she said.

"No thanks are necessary. We'll keep you posted on any further developments."

A few minutes later, Hope sat beside Gabe with Zeke lying by their feet.

"We should talk about when I'm going back to New York," she said. She dreaded bringing it up, but it was inevitable. Although she had a surprise for him, would he still feel the same way about her?

"Yeah, about that. Remember when I told you that I'd go back with you? I meant it. So if you go, I'm going too."

"What?"

"You heard me."

"But your job, your house, everything."

"Don't you want to go back to work at the firm?"

"I thought I did, but after everything that happened with Sam, I'm thinking of looking for another firm."

"Really?"

"And actually, I've been offered a job."

"That's awesome, Hope."

"Well, will you be as excited if I tell you that it's here. At the Trent Law Firm?"

His dark eyes widened and then he smiled. He pulled her up from her chair and wrapped his arms around her. "Seriously?"

"Yes, Gabe. I want to stay here with you if...."

"Wait, just wait." He shook his head. "You're invading my territory."

"How so?"

"Because you know that I love you. I love you more than I ever thought possible. Being with you has given me a different perspective on my priorities."

"I feel the same way," she said softly. "You know all about me, Gabe. I've opened up to you more than I have any other person in my entire life. You see me for the real me—all my flaws and baggage. But you don't judge. I can't imagine going back to New York City and leaving you here."

"Share your life with me, Hope. I want to plan a future with you."

"A future?"

"Hope Finch," he asked. "I know you've been through a lot in your past. And I will totally understand if you want to take things slowly. But for me, Hope, there is no one else. I don't want to rush you. We can take it one day at a time, but I don't want to make plans and set goals if you aren't in that picture. How do you feel about that?"

Zeke barked.

"I'd have it no other way."

When he pressed his lips to hers, she finally understood the meaning of unconditional love.

EXCERPT FROM TRIAL & TRIBULATIONS: A WINDY RIDGE LEGAL THRILLER

CHAPTER ONE

When managing partner Chet Carter called, you answered—and you answered promptly. Just yesterday Olivia Murray had been summoned to Chet's corner office and told to pack her bags for a new case that would take her from Washington, DC to the Windy Ridge suburb of Chicago.

But this wasn't just any case. She would be defending a New Age tech company called Astral Tech in a lawsuit filed by its biggest competitor.

As she stepped out of her red Jeep rental, the summer breeze blew gently against her face. She stared up at the mid sized office building with a prominent sparkling blue moon on the outside, and she had to admit she was a bit intimidated. It wasn't the litigation aspect that bothered her, though. It was the subject matter.

She threw her laptop bag over her shoulder, adjusted her black suit jacket, and walked toward the door. Ready for anything. Or at least she hoped she was.

The strong smell of incense hit her as her first heeled foot stepped through the door. She thought it was a bit cliché for a New Age company to be burning incense in the reception area, but maybe it was to be expected. It reinforced her thoughts that this was all a money making operation—not a group of actual believers in this stuff.

The perky young blonde behind the minimalist glass desk looked up at her. "How can I help you?"

"Hi, I'm Olivia Murray from the law firm of Brown, Carter, and Reed."

The young woman's brown eyes widened. "Oh, yes, Ms. Murray. I'm Melanie." She stood and shook Olivia's hand. "Let me know if you need anything while you're here. The team is expecting you. I'll take you to the main conference room now."

"Thank you." Everything was already proceeding as normal. She couldn't let this whole New Age thing mess with her head. And besides that, she had her faith to get her through this.

Melanie led her down the hall to a conference room and knocked loudly before opening the large door. "Ms. Murray, please go on in."

Olivia didn't really know what she expected, but what she saw was a table full of suits arguing. She let out a breath. Regular litigation. Just like she had thought.

A man stood up from the table. "You must be our lawyer from BCR?" He wore an impeccably tailored navy suit with a red tie. He had short dark hair with a little gray at the temples and piercing green eyes.

"Yes, I'm Olivia Murray."

"Great. This is the Astral Tech leadership team. Don't let our yelling worry you. That's how we best communicate." He laughed. "I'm Clive Township, the CEO of Astral Tech, and this is my trusted inner circle."

A striking woman rose and offered her hand. "I'm Nina Marie Crane, our Chief Operating Officer."

"Wonderful to meet you," Olivia said.

Clive nodded toward a tall thin man with black hair who stood and shook her hand. "And this is our financial voice of reason, Matt Tinley."

"I serve as our Chief Financial Officer," Matt said.

Everyone greeted her warmly, but she felt an undercurrent of tension in the room. It was now her job as their attorney to get this litigation under control and that also meant getting them under control. Half the battle of litigation was controlling your own client before you could even begin to take on the adversary.

"Have a seat and we'll get you up to speed," Clive said.

She sat down in a comfortable dark blue chair at the oblong oak table and pulled out her laptop to take any relevant notes. She opened up her computer, but mainly she wanted to get the lay of the land.

"So the more I can learn about your company and the complaint that Optimism has filed against you the better. One of the first things I'll have to work on is the document collection and fact discovery effort. To be able to do that, I need the necessary background. I'll be happy to go over the discovery process with you, too, at some point so we're all on the same page."

"Where do you want to start?" Nina Marie asked.

"It would be helpful if you gave me a more detailed explanation of your company. I did my own research, but I'd love to hear it from you. Then we can move onto the legal claims brought against you by Optimism."

"Nina Marie is the driving force behind Astral Tech. So I'll let her explain our business," Clive said. "I'm more of the big picture guy and Matt is our number cruncher."

"Sounds good," Olivia said.

Nina Marie smiled. The thin auburn haired woman wore tortoiseshell glasses. Her hair was swept up into a loose bun, and she wore a black blazer with a rose colored blouse. "Astral Tech was my baby, but Clive has the financial backing and business acumen to make it happen."

"I'd like to hear all about it," Olivia said.

"We're a company specializing in bringing New Age theories and ideas into the tech space. We felt like we filled a void in that area. Yes, New Age has been quite popular for years now, but no company has really brought New Age into the current technology arena and made it work for the next generation. Through the Astral Tech app and other electronic means, we're making New Age relevant again. Our target audience is youth and young professionals. We don't even try to reach the baby boomers and beyond because it's a losing battle. They're too traditional, and they're not as tech savvy. We have to target our energy on the demographic that makes the most sense for our product."

"Excuse my ignorance, but you use New Age as a blanket term. I need a bit of education on what exactly you mean in the context of your business."

Nina Marie clasped her hands together in front of her. "Of course. I think a woman like you is in our key demographic. I would love to hear your thoughts on all of this. But to answer your question, New Age is a lot more than incense and meditation, although that is definitely a part of it. New Age is a way of life. A way of spiritually connecting. We care about the whole body—the environment, mysticism, spirituality. And we do that in an innovative way through the Astral Tech app that starts you on your path of self exploration from day one. You have to download it and try it for yourself. It will definitely help you understand our issues in the litigation better."

"Yes, the litigation. I read the complaint on the plane. Optimism's central claim is that Astral Tech actually stole the app from them."

Clive jumped in and leaned forward resting his arms on the table. "It's a totally bogus lawsuit. That's why we're hiring a firm like yours to nip this in the bud. We don't want any copycat litigation. This app was developed totally in house by Astral Tech employees. To say that there is any theft is absolutely false. We certainly didn't steal it. It's just a trumped up charge."

"What about the other claim regarding defamation?"

Clive nodded. "The defamation claim is actually a bit more concerning to me because it's subjective. We won't have a technical expert that can testify about that like we have on the actual theft claim."

She sat up in her seat. "What was said by Astral Tech that they are claiming is defamatory?"

"A few off handed comments about Optimism and their lack of integrity. They claim they're part of the New Age movement, but some of their actions indicate otherwise."

"Could you be more specific?"

"I can elaborate," Nina Marie said. "Optimism isn't really centered on New Age techniques in the same way we are. Their original founder, Earl Ward, was a connoisseur of many New Age techniques, but when he passed away Optimism's purpose shifted a bit under Layton Alito's rule, solidifying their allegiance to the dark arts. Layton is a ruthless leader who doesn't tolerate any type of dissent amongst his ranks."

Olivia felt her eyes widen, but she tried to hide her surprise. "Are you serious?"

"Yes, very," Nina Marie said.

"And Astral Tech isn't like that?" She couldn't help herself. She had to ask. It was better to know.

"We're a big tent. We don't want to alienate anyone who is seeking a spiritual journey," Clive said.

Well, that wasn't exactly a denial. What had she stepped into here? "And why New Age?"

Clive smiled. "Think about this as a lawyer. A businessperson. The world is becoming more and more open minded about spirituality. Which is obviously a good thing. Let everyone do what they want. We're moving away from strict codes of morality to something that fits with the modern person in this country. It's in. It's now. That's why we do it. We're using principles that have been popular for the past few decades and bringing them into the tech arena."

"For some of us, it's more than just about what makes money and make sense," Nina Marie said. "I'm proud to say that I'm a believer. A strong spiritual being. Those things have value. What we're doing matters. We have the ability to revolutionize the way people think about New Age principles."

Olivia could feel Nina Marie's dark eyes on her trying to evaluate whether she was truly friend or foe. A strange uneasiness settled over her. There was more to all of this than Nina Marie was saying. This was much larger than a lawsuit. Spiritual forces were at work here.

Focusing on the task at hand, she stared at her laptop and the page of notes she'd typed while hearing her clients talk. "I'll need to make sure you have a proper litigation hold in place to collect all relevant documents. I'll also want to talk to your IT person on staff right away about preserving all documents. The last thing we want to do is play cute and get sanctioned by the court. If Astral Tech has nothing to hide, then there's no reason to be evasive."

"But that's the thing," Matt said. "We believe we haven't broken any laws, but we also believe in our privacy and that of our customers."

Olivia nodded. "We should be able to petition the court for a protective order for any sensitive information that is turned over in the litigation, including customer lists. That's something we can handle."

Nina Marie stood up from her chair. "Let me take you to the office space we have set up for you while you're working here on this case."

"Thank you." While she was eager to get to work, she wasn't so excited about being alone with Nina Marie. But she followed the woman out of the conference room and down the hall, reminding herself that Nina Marie was still the client.

Nina Marie stopped abruptly about half way down the corridor. "I know this will sound a bit strange, but I'm getting a really interesting vibe from you."

"Vibe?"

"Yes. Do you have any interest in learning more about New Age spirituality? Anything like that?"

"No. That's not really my thing." She held back her direct answer which would've been totally unprofessional. She didn't feel comfortable in this environment, but she was also torn between her job and her faith. Could she really do both? Would defending a company like Astral Tech really be possible?

Conflicted feelings shot through her. No, she didn't believe in aliens or monsters, but she definitely believed in good and evil. Angels and demons. And this entire situation seemed like a recipe for disaster.

"I'm not giving up on you." Nina Marie reached out and patted her shoulder.

Nina Marie was quite a few inches taller than her, but that wasn't saying much considering she was only five foot three in heels.

"Once you learn more about our product offerings, I think you'll be excited to hear more about what we can do for a strong and smart professional woman like you."

"I appreciate your interest, Nina Marie, but my chief concern and responsibility is the lawsuit. So I think it'd be best if we could concentrate on that."

Nina Marie quirked an eyebrow but didn't immediately respond. Olivia followed her into another conference room, but this one was set up with multiple computer workstations around the large table. The rest of the décor matched the previous room they were in.

"This will be the legal work room for you. You should have plenty of space for everything you need in here."

"This is a great workspace." She looked around the room and was pleased by the size and technical accommodations. "I'm sure I'm going to run into a lot of factual questions as we start preparing for this first phase of litigation. Who is the person at Astral Tech I should go to with questions?"

"That would be me for pretty much anything that is detail oriented about the company or the app. Clive is good on the general business and philosophy but not so much on details. He's also not in the office everyday like I am. Matt can also serve as a resource both on the financial aspects and the spiritual ones."

"Got it." She'd never worked on such a strange case in her seven plus years of practicing law. Thankfully, she was steadfast in her beliefs. She just hoped that nothing in this litigation would require her to do things that went against her faith. Because she'd have to draw that line somewhere. And if it was a choice between her career or her faith, she'd always choose her faith.

***

Grant Baxter reviewed the document requests he had drafted one last time. He enjoyed being on the plaintiff's side of the table—even if it was for an odd client. Some wacky New Age group had retained his small but reputable law firm to sue Astral Tech—an equally wacky company in his opinion.

He didn't have any time for religion whether it be traditional or New Age or whatever. To him it was all just a convenient fiction made up to help people deal with their fears and insecurities. But if this case would help his firm take the next steps to success and keep paying the bills, then he was all for it.

He'd built his law firm, The Baxter Group, from the ground up—something he was very proud of, given all his long hours and sacrifices. Not a thing in his life had been given to him. He'd earned it all the hard way.

He couldn't help but chuckle as he read over the document requests that he had prepared. All the talk of witches and spirituality and the Astral Tech app. He'd never drafted anything like that before. His law school classes and nine years of practice had equipped him with many skills, but working on a case like this was totally foreign to him.

It wasn't like there were witches in a coven out to get him. People were entirely irrational when it came to religion. Luckily for him, he wasn't one of those people. He might be the only sane person in the entire litigation, and he planned to stay that way. One thing he was certain about. A jury was going to eat this stuff up.

"Hey, boss man." Ryan Wilde stood at Grant's door.

"What's going on?" Grant asked.

"I asked around town trying to find info on Astral Tech, but most of my contacts had never heard of them, and the few that had didn't really have anything useful to say except that they're trying to become players in the tech space."

Ryan was only about two years younger than Grant. They'd both worked in a law firm together for years, and Grant was glad that Ryan had joined him at the firm. If all progressed as planned, Grant was going to add Ryan as his partner in the firm.

"If you do hear anything, just let me know."

"Anything else you need from me?"

"Not on this. How are your other cases going?"

"I'm meeting with potential clients this afternoon on a products liability class action. It would be a good case to have."

"Keep me posted."

Ryan nodded. "You got it." Ryan walked out the door and then turned around and laughed. "I have to say, I'm glad that you're working this case and not me. I don't think I'd know how to approach it."

"Just like anything else. It'll be fine."

"If you say so. I hope you don't end up with a hex put on you or something like that."

Grant laughed. "Don't even tell me that you would consider believing in any of this."

Ryan shook his head. "Nah. I'm just messing with you."

Ryan walked out and Grant was anxious to start the discovery process and put pressure on the other side. It was one of those things he loved about being a plaintiff's lawyer. He was in the driver's seat and planned to take an aggressive stance in this case to really turn the heat up on the other side. Going through these steps reminded him how glad he was that he went out and started his own firm. He truly loved his work.

His office phone rang, jerking him back to reality.

"This is Grant Baxter," he said.

"Hello. My name is Olivia Murray from the law firm of Brown, Carter, and Reed. I just wanted to call to introduce myself. We're representing Astral Tech in the suit filed by your client. So I'll be your point of contact for anything related to the case."

Well, well he thought. Astral Tech had gone and hired a high powered law firm based in Washington, DC to defend them. "Perfect timing. I was just getting ready to send out discovery requests for documents. BCR doesn't have a Chicago office, right?"

"No, but I'm actually in town. I'm working at the client's office in Windy Ridge. So you can send any hard copies of anything to the Astral Tech office, and I would appreciate getting everything by email also." She rattled off her email address.

"Of course. And I have the feeling we'll be talking a lot. This litigation is going to be fast tracked if my client has anything to say about it. We're not going to just wait around for years letting things pass us by."

She laughed. "Yes, I know how it is. I'll look forward to your email."

He hung up and leaned back in his chair. Know thy enemy, right? He immediately looked her up on the Internet finding her BCR firm profile. A brunette with big brown eyes smiled back at him. He read her bio. Impressive, double Georgetown girl. Seventh year associate at BCR where she'd spent her entire legal career. That would make her about two years younger than him— but definitely still a seasoned attorney and worthy opponent.

Astral Tech wasn't messing around. That let him know that they took this litigation seriously. They didn't see this as a nuisance suit. Game on.

***

"Do you think Olivia's ready for this fight?" Micah asked Ben looking directly into his dark eyes.

"It doesn't matter if she's really ready, Micah. It's a battle she has to fight and the time is now. We have no one else. She's the one God has chosen who has to stand up and take this on. She has some idea that she's meant to be here. But it might take her a little time to figure out exactly what she's going to be involved with."

The angels stood behind Olivia watching over her in the conference room. But she hadn't sensed their presence as she continued to type away on her laptop and hum a tune.

"She isn't fully appreciative of how strong she is, but she'll get there," Micah said. He stood tall, his blond hair barely touching his shoulders. The angel warrior was strong but kind—and fiercely protective of Olivia.

Ben nodded. "At least she has the foundation to build upon. A strong faith that has been growing ever since she was a little girl." Ben paused. "Unlike our friend Grant."

"I'm much more worried about him. He has no idea what he's going to be facing, and he doesn't have the skills to defend himself. Nina Marie and her followers are building up strength by the day, and she'll surely want to go after him. We can only do so much to protect Olivia and Grant against the forces of evil running rampant on this earth."

"But we'll do everything we can."

Micah looked at him. "You and me—quite an angel army."

"The best kind."

"Let's pray for her now."

The two laid their hands on her shoulders to help prepare her for the fight to come. A fight unlike anything they'd ever known before.

EXCERPT FROM EXPERT WITNESS

CHAPTER ONE

"**A**ll rise." The bailiff's deep voice echoed through the crowded Atlanta courtroom.

Sydney Berry took a deep breath and stepped down from the witness stand. Unfortunately, her expert testimony as a forensic artist in the murder trial of businessman Kevin Diaz wasn't over. She'd have to come back tomorrow and testify about her sessions with the eyewitness and the drawing she'd created of the suspect. The goal—to get the sketch of the suspect introduced into evidence. It would bolster the eyewitness testimony to have the contemporaneous drawing in front of the jury.

If the defense attorney was able to tear apart her testimony, the prosecution's case would be severely weakened. And a guilty man likely would walk free. She refused to let that happen.

She walked out of the courtroom doors, and then the other bailiff standing outside nodded to her, indicating she was on her own. *Dear God, please give me the strength to get through this. Let my testimony help the jury so that justice may be done for the murder of an innocent woman.*

"Ms. Berry!" A male voice rang out down the courthouse hallway.

The last thing she wanted to do right now was deal with the press. She'd refused every media inquiry thus far, and she would do the same again today. Because of Kevin Diaz's position in the community, the local Atlanta media were having a field day covering the trial.

"No comment." She turned around and came face to face with a tall man in a dark suit and a navy checkered tie. No, he didn't look like the press. He had to be a Fed. His dark brown hair was cut short, and his eyes were a striking deep green.

"I'm not a reporter," he said. "Please let me escort you to your vehicle, and I'll explain."

She took a step, and he followed her.

She turned to him. "Who are you?"

He looked her in the eyes. "I'm US Marshal Max Preston."

Close. She had figured him for FBI. Having dealt with the FBI quite a bit in her line of work, she knew its style, and he fit it perfectly down to the gun she caught a glimpse of on his right hip. Though she wasn't accustomed to consulting for the US Marshals, they were obviously built from the same mold.

"As you can tell, I'm a bit preoccupied right now with this trial." She reached into her pocket for her business card. "Here's my card. Contact me and we can set up a consultation. But it will probably be a few weeks before I can fit it into my schedule." When he refused the card, she pocketed it and pushed open the courthouse door. The summer heat of Atlanta hit her, and she already felt her hair starting to frizz.

"I know this is bad timing, but I need five minutes," he said, following her outside.

The persistent marshal wasn't taking no for an answer. They walked down the courthouse steps on to the sidewalk.

"Really, sir, this isn't a good time."

He touched her arm. "It's important, Ms. Berry. I wouldn't come to you like this otherwise, but I really need to talk to you. Now."

Then she heard car wheels screeching loudly. Looking toward the street, she saw a dark SUV barreling down the road in their direction at top speed. Instinctively, she took a step back.

The tinted window rolled down, and the sound of gunshots exploded through the air. Before she could duck, she found herself hitting the sidewalk hard and tasted the faint taste of blood in her mouth.

Screams and mass chaos erupted around her. As she looked up trying to determine what had happened, she realized that the US marshal with the bright green eyes was on top of her, shielding her body with his own. He had knocked her down. Probably saving her life.

"That's what I wanted to talk to you about," he said quietly in her ear. "Are you okay?" He lifted his weight off her and his eyes scanned her from head to toe, as if looking for signs of injury.

"I'm fine." She paused, trying to catch her breath. "Wait a minute. You think those bullets were meant for me?"

He gently pulled her up off the ground and wrapped one arm around her shoulder to steady her. "Unfortunately, I do. I need to get you to a secure location. Now."

As police officers swarmed around them, he flashed his marshal's badge and was able to get through the crowd. He pulled one of the officers aside. "Neil, we need to talk."

"What happened here?" the officer asked him.

"Drive-by shooting. Approximately five shots fired. Two men, driver and passenger."

"Did you get a visual on either?"

"Negative, but they were in a black Chevy SUV—model year late nineties. I'm assuming it was stolen, and they're probably dumping the vehicle as we speak."

"You're probably right about that."

"Look, Neil, call me if you need anything else, but right now I need to get this witness out of here. When it's safe, we can provide official statements. Please keep me in the loop. You have my info."

The officer nodded at Max and then looked at her closely. Recognition spread across his face. He must have been following the Diaz trial. "Of course. Whatever you need, Max."

Max took her arm and led her down the street away from the courthouse. "I should try to explain why I came here today. I think you're in more danger than you could know."

"With that lead in, I guess you already know me pretty well."

"Yes, I do, Ms. Berry."

"Please, call me Sydney. After you saved my life I feel like the formalities are a bit much. Can I call you Max?"

"Of course."

"So what's going on exactly?"

He gently touched her back and guided her to his car, which he'd parked in the lot down the block from the courthouse. He opened the door, and she got into the nondescript gray sedan. Only then did he start to explain.

"I used to work in the gang unit at the FBI." He paused. "But I came here today to warn you that there was chatter amongst the gang networks about you. Have you ever heard of the East River gang?"

"Yeah, they're pretty notorious." She wasn't ready to provide her specific knowledge of the East River gang to this man she just met. Even if he had saved her life, she thought it better to proceed with caution. That was the way she lived now.

"Well, I put two and two together and I think the East River gang has decided to go after you because of your testimony here in the case against Kevin Diaz."

"Kevin Diaz is a businessman with multiple thriving companies. What connection could he possibly have to the East River gang?" She kept her voice steady even as her mind started to play out the implications of this new piece of information.

"Kevin's cousin is Lucas Jones who just happens to also be one of the power players in East River."

She looked over at him. "Wow. I had no idea they were related." She paused. "And now you think they're coming after me because of the family connection?"

"I'll be honest with you. I'm one of the only ones who believe that Lucas Jones would take action for his estranged cousin. Most of my former FBI colleagues believe that the two of them aren't on speaking terms. But I do and that's why I'm here. I had a feeling that East River would retaliate against you and today's events only confirm my hunch."

"Are you sure?"

He kept his eyes on the road. "I felt pretty strongly about it before, but you were almost gunned down in broad daylight outside the courthouse. So, yes, it's a threat I take seriously. The US Marshals' office is taking it seriously."

"What does all of this mean?"

"It means that for the time being you'll be in my protective custody. It was one thing when you were just testifying in a murder trial against Kevin Diaz. But circumstances have changed. If you're a target of the East River gang because of your testimony that impacts everything. First and foremost your personal safety. When you agreed to testify as an expert witness for the state, it wasn't under these circumstances."

She took a second and looked out the window as they drove. "Is all this really necessary?"

"Most people are thankful for the protection, Ms. Berry."

I can take care of myself, she thought. "It's Sydney, remember? And it's not that I'm not thankful. It's just that I'm having a hard time processing all of this. I'm not exactly used to being shot at when testifying in a major trial. Not to mention being told that I'm going to have my every move shadowed by someone I just met. I just need a few minutes to think it all through."

He nodded. "If you decide to continue to testify tomorrow, I'll make sure you are able to safely arrive and finish your testimony. Then we'll determine the next steps after that."

"What do you mean *if*? Why wouldn't I testify? I already committed to it."

"That was before you knew about the danger to your life. The prosecutor will have to talk to you about the risks involved. And then we'll need to lay low until there's a proper threat assessment conducted on the risk to your life from the East River gang."

She couldn't believe what she was hearing. "Wait. Are you talking about putting me into the witness protection program?"

"That would be premature at this juncture."

"But you're not ruling it out?"

"I never rule out any course of action. Doing so is the easiest way to get you or someone else killed. But the lead prosecutor and state's attorney are going to be fully briefed on the current security issues, and they may seek that route for you. Especially after what just happened."

"Unbelievable." She lived a solitary life so she didn't have to worry about a family, but this marshal was throwing her a curve. Granted, he was just doing his job, but that didn't mean she felt comfortable with him taking over. She was a private person. She'd only trusted a man once before, and she shuddered thinking about him.

"I know this is difficult for you. If it makes you feel any better, I'll do everything I can to keep you safe and try and give you as much space as is reasonable."

"I guess I understand. But how could the state not have known about this connection to the East River gang?"

"Since there isn't any proven contact or links between the two cousins, I don't think the state believed this was a relevant issue. Lucas thought Kevin sold out by working in corporate America. Or at least that's the story that's on the streets."

"But you're skeptical?"

"Yeah. I'm not doubting that there's friction between the two of them, but I don't buy for a minute that Kevin Diaz is completely on the up and up. The FBI is investigating his operations trying to find any other ties to East River or organized crime. However, it's not their top priority. Like I said, I was the one driving that charge, and now that I'm gone it's less of a focus. Regardless, in my opinion East River made clear today that they don't want you to testify."

"But I've already started my testimony."

"And they don't want you to finish it," he shot back. "You've only gotten through the preliminary questions. Nothing you've said so far will hurt Diaz. It's the rest of your testimony that would be problematic for him. So for tonight we have to be on lockdown. I'm taking you to a safe house in the area."

"I'll need something to wear for court tomorrow."

"Don't worry. All of that will be taken care of. We have a fully stocked safe house, and if need be we can send out for any additional necessities."

She leaned her head back against the seat and closed her eyes for a second trying to steady her ever escalating nerves. She liked to be in control, and right now things were spiraling quickly into a place she didn't like to be. *Lord, I need you now.*

"Are you all right?" he asked.

"Yes. How much farther until we reach our destination?"

"It's just outside the city, so only a few more minutes."

"Sorry to sound impatient."

He glanced over at her. "You were just shot at. You have every right to feel a mix of emotions. I'm actually quite impressed at how you've held yourself together."

She wanted to change the subject and take the focus off of her. "Are you from around here?" she asked.

"I'm from Chicago, but I've lived all over working for the FBI. For the past few years I worked out of the Atlanta field office. And now as a marshal, I've been assigned to the Northern District of Georgia."

"I like living in Atlanta," she said.

The car suddenly swerved, stopping her from continuing her thought. What was going on?

"Hold on," he said loudly.

She gripped onto the console.

Then he slammed on the brakes.

***

Max's day was going from bad to worse. If he hadn't gotten to the courthouse when he had, his witness might have been killed— gunned down in broad daylight. And now a man stood waving his arms right in front of his car in the middle of the road.

Max had to swerve to keep from hitting him. But it was close. And now his senses were screaming that something was terribly off. They were winding through the suburbs on the way to the safe house. What was this man doing?

He thought of Sydney. How much more could she handle today? She certainly hadn't signed up for being a target of the East River gang. His years in the FBI gang unit had shown him just how ruthless a group like East River could be.

"Are you going to get out and see what he needs?" she asked.

They sat in the car, not moving, as the man approached. Max estimated him to be in his forties, approximately six foot tall and two hundred pounds. He definitely didn't look like a damsel in distress.

"What's wrong?" she asked Max.

"I don't like this."

"He probably needs help." She reached over and grabbed his arm. "We can't just ignore him."

"Stay in the car, okay?"

Before she could answer, he checked his sidearm and then opened the door.

And that's when the man lunged forward. The attacker was fast, but Max was faster.

Sydney screamed, but Max stayed focused on the threat in front of him. But when a gunshot went off, he instinctively turned to look. And there was Sydney wrestling another man with a gun.

He didn't have time to do a thorough analysis of the situation, so he quickly launched into action. When his attacker landed a blow that connected hard with his jaw, pain shot through his head. But it wasn't enough to lay him out. There was no way was he going to lose his first official witness as a US Marshal. With a swift uppercut he made contact with the attacker's face. Calling on his martial arts training, he followed with a precise kick to the ribs. His assailant landed on the ground with a resounding thud.

He drew his gun and turned, ready to take the shot to save Sydney's life. But somehow she had gotten the other guy on his knees and the man's gun was now in her hand. How in the world had she managed that? "Keep that gun on him, Sydney."

"You don't have to worry about that," she said.

He pulled out his handcuffs and secured the original assailant. Then he walked over to her. The other man was on his knees with his hands in the air. He pulled out a second pair of cuffs from his jacket and put them on the perpetrator.

He would need to call this in ASAP, but he also needed to get Sydney to safety. What if others were coming? These guys could have been waiting for them. Which meant additional threats could be in the area.

He pulled out his cell and put in a call. Backup should only be a few minutes away. That would give him a moment with the suspects. He read them their rights since he didn't want to get caught in a legal snafu, and then he looked at the first man.

"Who sent you?"

"I'm not talkin." The man's blue eyes weren't filled with fear but determination. Clearly he was a hired gun.

Max walked over to where Sydney stood beside the other man. Her auburn hair had come loose from her ponytail. "You sure you're okay?" She looked shaken as she gripped her hands together, but after a moment answered him calmly.

"Yes."

He turned his attention to the man. "You got anything to say?"

The guy grunted, and Max took that as a no. No surprises there.

As they held the men at gunpoint he leaned in to her. "Where in the world did you learn to incapacitate an attacker like that?" He guessed her to be only about five feet four, but she was a powerhouse.

Her brown eyes were wide as she looked up at him. "Self-defense classes."

"That looked like a whole lot more than self-defense class."

She shifted her weight from one foot to the other. "I'd rather not talk about it."

He was intrigued. Sydney Berry had secrets. And if he was going to be able to keep her safe, he probably needed to find them out. But at the moment he was just glad that her first secret actually worked to their advantage.

He was kicking himself for taking his eyes off of her earlier. She was his first and only priority. Granted, she wasn't officially in the Witness Security Program, known commonly as witness protection, but he had been tasked to keep her safe until everything could be sorted out.

Sirens sounded in the distance. He looked at her. "Why don't you get in the car? I'll handle this, and then we can be on our way." She frowned but then got into the sedan.

A moment later the local police arrived, and Max filled them in on the specifics. He'd also looped in his FBI contact. Then he made the call he was dreading. Reporting this incident to his boss, Deputy Elena Sanchez, was hardly the way to make a good first impression, but he had no choice.

Then finally he was ready to hit the road with Sydney. But not to the original safe house. That was too risky now.

He wouldn't feel even an ounce better until Sydney had safely completed her testimony in the morning. And even then the threat of the East River gang still loomed large.

Once they'd been driving for a few minutes, he decided to break the silence. "Want to talk about what happened back there?"

"You think those men were connected to East River or someone else associated with Diaz?"

He decided it best to be open and honest with her about the threat. "I think East River has put a hit out on you."

"I had a feeling you were going to say that," she said.

He saw her look out the window and take note of her surroundings. "I know it seems like I'm driving in the other direction now, but given what just happened we're going to an alternative safe house."

"But we're not staying there long?"

"No. After you testify we'll go to another location. This is just for tonight. We have a list of safe house options already planned for you."

"I guess I don't get much of a say in this, huh?"

"You always have a say, but you should know that I have your best interests in mind. Also, I'm sorry about what happened back there, however, I'm thankful that you were able to defend yourself."

"Me too," she said quietly.

He looked over at her. As she stared out the window he could see the tension tightening her features. He tried a different topic of conversation. "How long have you been a sketch artist?"

She turned to look at him, and her shoulders immediately seemed to relax. "I've been drawing forever, but I started taking it seriously during college. I didn't finish school and instead took art classes with my tuition money. Then I started with small jobs and it grew from there. Referrals are very important in my business. But I do more than just draw faces. That's what you think of when you think of a sketch artist. I'm a forensic artist. I can do a lot more, like crime scene re-enactments and stuff like that."

"I imagine the work comes and goes." He wanted to engage in conversation to try to calm his own building nerves, as well.

"Yes. I've been very busy as of late, but those first few years were tough. I took other odd jobs to make ends meet. I worked at a library for a bit and as a server at a restaurant. All to pursue my real dream." She shrugged. "With all the high-tech advancements, the field is changing a lot, it's really exciting. Computers can do a lot, but there's still something to be said about a human hand."

"I'm a big fan of using technology in investigations. I had an experience with a traditional sketch artist in the past who wasn't on point." That was an understatement, but he didn't think it was the best time to go into his misgivings about sketch artists right now.

"Don't get me wrong. The technology for doing things like facial reconstructions or accident simulations is absolutely amazing," she replied. "But I still trust my abilities to use pencil and paper and sketch based on the eyewitness interview for the purposes of identification."

He didn't reply because it only would have led to an argument that he didn't think she would want to have right now.

"You said you were at the FBI before. How long have you been a marshal?"

He didn't really want to give an exact answer. "Not very long."
He could feel her gaze on him as he drove.

"Hey, don't tell me I'm your first witness."

He smiled. "Okay, I won't tell you that."

"Wow." She blew out a breath. "I *am* your first witness."

"That's true, but I'd been with the FBI for a decade. It's not like
I'm new to law enforcement, so I'm not a true rookie."

"I can imagine that working as an FBI agent in the gang unit
is a lot different than guarding a witness, though."

"Don't give it another thought. You're safe now, and you'll
stay that way."

"No offense, but we just met. You're asking me to put a lot of
faith in you."

"I know. But that's the way it has to be. No one else on our team
has the same knowledge of the threats to you like I do. I'm thankful
that I got assigned to your case and was able to connect the dots, or
this afternoon might have ended very differently." He paused as he
pointed to a house up ahead. "We're here on the right."

"This looks like a regular neighborhood."

"That's exactly the point. We're trying to blend."

He'd actually never been to this safe house before during his
training, but he was getting the idea that they were all generally
the same. This was a two-story house, painted a pale blue on a
nice size lot.

He pulled the sedan all the way into the driveway and stopped
the car.

"Can I get out?" she asked.

"Yes, but first let me just do a quick security check. You stay
here and keep the doors locked."

Before she could answer he had jogged up to the front door
and opened it. He quickly surveyed the house, conducting a
security sweep. Satisfied it was all clear he went back outside to
get Sydney. Her expression appeared unreadable as she sat in the

passenger's seat. He really wanted to know what was going in that head of hers.

He opened the car door for her, and she stepped out bedside him. She was a pretty woman, no doubt, with a simple and natural beauty about her. But she gave off a very strong vibe. One that said loudly, "Back off."

"This way," he said. He took her arm and escorted her to the front door, even though he got the feeling she didn't appreciate him invading her personal space. "Another marshal will be over in a bit with dinner and everything you'll need for tonight and tomorrow."

"You aren't leaving, are you?" she asked as she made direct eye contact.

"No. I just didn't want you to think we were going to be totally shut off from the outside world without the things you would need."

"What I really need is to be at my own home."

"I understand. Let's get through your testimony in the morning, and then we can re-evaluate."

"I'll hold you to that."

He walked over to where she stood in the living room. "I promise. And I won't make you promises I can't keep. I hate it when people do that to me and—"

A loud crash rocked the room as glass flew against his body. His face burned and he felt blood trickling down his cheek. Smoke surrounded him. He dove toward Sydney, hoping it wouldn't be too late.

EXCERPT FROM
OUT OF HIDING

Sadie felt the bullet whiz by her head as she crouched down in the wet dirt. Darkness surrounded her, but she wasn't alone. Her gut screamed loudly that something was terribly wrong. And she always trusted her gut. She had company, and if that bullet was any indication, they meant business. The sound of the crackling leaves told her someone was moving quickly in her direction.

Dressed in all black, she lay flat on the ground in the dark woods. No one was going to see her. That bullet wasn't meant for her but was intended for someone else. Who? She didn't want to stick around long enough to find out. She prayed that Megan wasn't out here in the woods tonight—alone, scared, and with bullets flying. It was no place for a sixteen-year-old girl.

She checked her gun and kept her position low against the damp, muddy ground. Her night vision goggles were a blessing. It was then she saw what she dreaded the most. The letters FBI on a dark-colored flak jacket as an agent trounced his way through the woods. Why the FBI was involved in whatever was happening in these woods she didn't know, but she didn't like it. They were invading her turf.

Sadie had her first solid lead on the Vladimir network in El Paso, and she didn't want to give up the opportunity. She'd been on stakeouts for weeks, desperately trying to determine if Igor—the man who had taken everything from her—was in El Paso. Her intel had been that something related to the Vladimir crew was going down in the woods tonight. She had hoped that whatever it was wasn't going to involve Megan—the missing girl she was looking for. Sadie knew that Vladimir's crew was responsible for her disappearance. That's why she'd sought out the job just days ago.

Technically, she was still in the Witness Security Program commonly known as Witness Protection, although they didn't consider her to be in immediate danger anymore. She'd followed all their rules over the years. Her new life, her new name, everything. Done by the book. Not a single deviation from the protocol given to her by the U.S. Marshals. There was no way she'd let them know what she planned to do now that she had confirmation Igor sought to set up shop in her own backyard. It was only a matter of time before Witness Protection realized Igor's activities had expanded down to El Paso, and then they'd want her to move. She needed to act fast if she had any chance of taking out Igor's network.

She slowly stood up using a large tree as a shield. Thankfully, she was small of stature. By the time she'd registered the crunch of a stick right behind her it was too late. A large hand grabbed her shoulder with another muffling her scream.

"FBI, don't move," the deep voice said directly into her ear.

Didn't matter who he was, when a man put his hands on her, he was going to pay. She'd trained for moments like these. She slammed her foot down on his, and he groaned. But he didn't loosen his grip. Was this guy made of iron?

Trying another approach, she went limp in his arms, shocking him into loosening his grip, giving her a moment to slide away. She'd only taken two steps when he tackled her, knocking her to the ground. She could barely breathe. She squirmed against him, but she was no match for his size and strength. He had to have been at least a foot taller and a hundred pounds heavier. For a moment, fear seized her. She said a prayer asking God to keep her safe and then fought back.

"Stop struggling," he said quietly, his voice steady. "I promise I'm not going to hurt you."

She didn't believe him. She knew better than to trust the Feds. Trust them, and she could end up dead like her parents. He adjusted his grip just enough for her to knee him in the stomach. Big mistake on her part. Now he seemed raving mad.

"I'm trying to save your life here. You have no idea what you've gotten yourself into. You should not be here in these woods right now."

The thing was, she actually wasn't a stranger to life-and-death situations. So this one didn't faze her too much. "I already dodged one bullet and was doing just fine on my own."

"You'll have time later to explain how you ended up in the middle of an active FBI investigation packing heat and wearing night vision goggles. For now, let me get you out of here safe and sound."

She shuddered. Those promises had been made to her before. And they'd been broken—every single one of them.

"I'm not going anywhere with you," she hissed. She struggled against his secure grip.

"Yes, you are, ma'am. Listen to me." He paused, his breathing ragged. "Things are only going to get worse. You might not be as fortunate the next time a bullet gets fired. And I don't want to have your death on my conscience. I have enough guilt to last a lifetime. So when I say three, we move for that next tree. You hear me?"

Realizing her current options were limited, she relented. He was right. Her best move for now was to retreat. She'd taken a taxi tonight and made her way to the woods on foot. It wasn't as if she had her own ride out of danger. She'd have time to get away from him once they got to safety. "Okay."

"One, two, three, go go go!" he said in a low voice. They sprinted from their current position to the next tree and squatted down. That's when she heard another round of gunfire. Automatic weapons this time. Her heartbeat quickened, but now was not the time to panic. She'd been in worse situations without the valuable experience that she now carried with her after years of being a private investigator.

"What next?" she whispered, trying to catch her breath.

"Make a run for that far tree. My Jeep is beyond it. I'm hoping that will work."

"And if not?"

"I'll think of plan B."

He sounded so sure of himself. Typical for FBI types. She wasn't going to count on him to get her out of here safely. She'd survey her options once they made it to the next tree before she jumped in the Jeep of a total stranger—even if he was in the FBI. Hadn't she already learned that tough lesson?

"Now," he barked.

She ran ahead of him using her small size and speed to her advantage, making it to the tree first. Though he wasn't far behind. She saw the dark Jeep parked behind a cluster of trees providing them with additional cover.

"Let's go for it," he said.

Making a split second decision that she prayed she wouldn't regret, she slid into the passenger side and ducked down low. Before she could even steady herself, the FBI guy had turned the ignition and floored it. The bumpy ride had her on high alert as he navigated the vehicle over the rough terrain.

She stayed down not knowing if they were safe from the gunfire and started plotting her escape. No way was she being taken in by the FBI to "explain herself."

They drove a few minutes in silence as the Jeep weaved through the wooded area and onto the country road that would eventually lead back into town. Then he spoke after checking his mirrors. "We're in the clear."

She eased up into her seat and looked around at her surroundings, including the man driving. She wasn't wrong in her initial assessment. This guy was tall and bulky. She already knew from the encounter in the woods that he was strong. His brown hair was cut short. She couldn't see his eyes since they were focused on what lay ahead. She told herself to remember that he was one of them.

He glanced over at her. "You want to tell me now what you were doing out in the woods?"

"My job," she snapped. Who knows what he thought she was doing, but her answer was completely truthful.

"And what job is that?"

She sighed, already not enjoying this line of questioning. "I'm a private investigator."

"You're not plugged into our FBI investigation, though. I would've known it."

"I have no idea what investigation you're working on." She let out a deep breath and figured she needed to provide an explanation. Maybe it would help her get away from him sooner. "I was in the woods searching for a missing girl. You may have even seen a local news story about her. Her mother recently hired me. I've been looking everywhere. I didn't see or hear anything until I felt the first bullet whiz by my ear." She was telling the truth. She had to make sure Megan wasn't in those woods tonight. It appeared that her leads had been correct. Something was going on with the Vladimir crew. And the FBI was involved. She said another silent prayer for Megan.

"Wow," he said. "You were in the wrong place at the wrong time, Ms. P.I. lady. I'm going to need to bring you in, though. Gotta take your statement. Make it official." His southern drawl was unmistakable.

"I don't think that's a good idea."

"I promise it'll be quick. You are carrying a weapon. I assume you have a permit for that and all."

No way she'd allow him to take her in, but she didn't have to tell him that. Her past struggles with the FBI were her own. Better to have the element of surprise.

"Uh, oh," he said. He jerked the wheel hard to the right sending her into his right arm. "We've got company. Hold on."

"I thought you said we were good."

"They came out of nowhere."

She turned around and saw a large dark SUV that was gaining on them. But FBI guy had some moves and was taking the curves on the dark country road with finesse as he drove toward the more populated area of town.

"Who are these people?" she asked as she clenched her fists. Were they connected to Vladimir?

"The less you know the better."

"Why don't you let me take a shot? I could probably blow out their tire."

"You're that good of a shot?" he asked with disbelief dripping from his deep voice.

"You better believe it," she said without hesitation.

He paused for a second and glanced over at her. "If you think you can, then go for it."

She was going to show this FBI guy that she was no slouch. In fact, she could probably outshoot him. All the time she'd spent at the range over the past few years had paid off. She turned around and was glad they were in a Jeep. Granted it didn't provide them with much, if any, protection, but it also meant she'd have an easier time getting off an unobstructed shot.

Steadying herself she took a deep breath, aimed, and pulled the trigger. It only took one shot, and the right front tire of the car chasing them was done for. The pursuit ended abruptly as they began to skid, the car circling in on the blown tire. "Got 'em."

"Well, Ms. P.I. lady, I'm impressed."

"You should be." Then she turned the gun toward him.

"Whoa." He lifted up his right hand at her while keeping his left on the wheel. "Just put that thing away."

Her hand was steady. "I have no reason to use this on you. But I'm not being taken in for questioning. I didn't do anything wrong."

"I never accused you of anything," he said with a raised voice. She watched as his hands tightened on the wheel.

"Take me downtown. Let me out and drive away. It's that simple."

"You're crazy, ma'am."

"No. But I'm the one with the gun right now, so I hope you don't try anything crazy."

"You're hiding something."

"It's none of your concern. Just act like you never saw me tonight."

"You know that's not possible. I'll have to write up this whole thing."

"Be creative," she countered. "Now let's get downtown. And don't try anything because I'd really hate to shoot you."

He let out a deep breath but started driving toward town as she directed. Good, she thought. She doubted that he'd let her go indefinitely. But she needed to get away and deal with this problem on her own terms. That meant not being taken in for questioning by the FBI tonight. She needed time.

When they reached the more crowded streets of downtown El Paso, she was ready to get away from him. "Slow down. Let me out. And keep on driving. Do you hear me?"

"Yes," he said in an even voice.

"Good."

He did as she asked and slowed down. She never took the gun off of him as she opened the door slowly. With the light from the streets flooding in, she could see his eyes were light blue. And questioning. "Just pretend I was never here. For your own good and mine too, okay?"

She couldn't shake the thought that she'd seen him before. She backed out of the Jeep, and he didn't say anything in response. She slammed the door shut, and he pulled away. She didn't waste any time weaving her way through the Saturday night crowd.

She was safe for now, but she had no doubt. The FBI guy would find her, and when he did, she'd be in a ton of trouble.

ABOUT RACHEL DYLAN

Rachel Dylan writes Christian fiction including inspirational romantic suspense for Love Inspired Suspense and the Windy Ridge Legal Thriller series. Rachel has practiced law for almost a decade and enjoys weaving together legal and suspenseful stories. She lives in Michigan with her husband and five furkids--two dogs and three cats. Rachel loves to connect with readers.

Connect with Rachel:
www.racheldylan.com
@dylan_rachel
www.facebook.com/RachelDylanAuthor

Made in the USA
Middletown, DE
28 February 2016